HEATHER JONES

THE
ROCK

© Heather Jones 2021

First edition published 2019
Second edition 2021
ISBN: 978-0-6452497-6-7 (sc)
ISBN: 978-0-6452497-5-0 (ebk)

This novel is a work of fiction. Names, characters, places, and incidents are either products of the author's imagination or used fictitiously. All characters are fictional, and any similarity to people living or dead is purely coincidental.

A CiP entry is available from the National Library of Australia

Published in conjunction with DoctorZed Publishing
W: www.doctorzed.com
E: info@doctorzed.com

rev. date 16/08/2021

DEDICATION

For Clare, Grace, Helen,

Doris, Mavis & Thelma

CHAPTER ONE

Nothing stirred in the cave on the tiny rocky islet, separated from the larger island by the angry Aegean Sea. Quiet, dry and warm it was in soothing contrast to conditions outside. Roaring surf would have drowned out conversation if there had been any between those gathered below on the beach.

Two male shipwreck survivors stood in rags, and four women, dressed in white habits, with their skirts drawn up between their legs like huge pantaloons and tightly secured around the waist, waited anxiously.

'What are they waiting for?' Christos, the younger man, huskily whispered. Tomas shrugged, he had no idea what they were waiting for but guessed it was to do with the boat.

'I think we are going somewhere,' Tomas managed to croak, and immediately received a sharp jab in the ribs from one of the women who covered her mouth and frowned severely at him.

Little did the men know the women were waiting for 'the sign', and all kept their backs turned to the cave, not wanting to look up, for fear of what they might see.

Inside the cave it was as if there had been no human habitation for months. A narrow entrance opened into a wide cavern, the centre of which was occupied by a fireplace. Along one side of the cavern stood a rough bench formed by a large flat stone balanced across two piles of smaller stones, it was stacked with a few clay bowls, a large clay jar of water and another of cornmeal, plus a few eating utensils. The faintest trace of herbal salve emanated from the back of the cave, where almost unnoticeable, a still form lay on a pile of dry seaweed, covered by a thick grey blanket.

The big island appeared to be no more than a huge rock presenting a sheer face, offering no foothold or sanctuary and yet it was in this direction the women stared. Miraculously, a sign did appear. Un-noticed by the men a thin thread of light shimmered intermittently upon the surface of the sea, disappearing for long seconds between waves and then suddenly re-appearing. It galvanised the women who expertly launched their sturdy wooden boat and indicated for the men to climb aboard. The light was no more than moonlight fragmenting with the movement of the water but, none the less, showed the seafarers the run of the tide and the shift of the channel they were to follow. Two of the women stood in the knee-high surf holding the boat steady while the others took up their positions. It was a difficult manoeuvre, made more so by their cumbersome attire, which was now wet and heavy, but they accomplished it quickly. They were soon embroiled in their battle to keep to their course. All the while, not one word was spoken.

Not having the strength to do otherwise, Tomas and Christos put their trust in the women who rowed through the rough conditions, heading straight for the great rock. Now they were dangerously close to the jagged teeth of a reef that looked as if it would cut them to pieces. The women pulled hard to the left on their oars, then harder again hitting a channel that flung them forward until they burst into the calmer waters of the inner reef. They rowed in silence close to the base of the rock. It towered above them in black menace offering no harbour. So close were they now that the women on the port side were using their oars to keep the boat from smashing against it. A narrow chasm appeared, its entry screened by an old rock slide. One of the women signalled and all crouched down low. The men swiftly copied the action. Carried forward by its own impetus, the boat bumped through the narrow opening then slipped quietly into a vast inky cavern. Resuming upright positions, the men, once accustomed to the gloom, noticed with amazement two or three small boats moored in the cave. Emerging from the cavern, they were further amazed to see a tiny ancient harbour, one whose beginnings must surely be lost in the mists of time.

A lone woman with stark white hair, also dressed in a white habit and looking ghostly in the moonlight, stood on the stone dock. She raised her hand. No-one spoke until they were moored, unloaded and assembled before her. She addressed the two men.

'Welcome to Luminos, our home. ' She paused, seeing how startled they were at being addressed in their own language. She held up her hand, this time to silence them and their rush of questions, she had that authority. Tomas had opened his mouth, but no sound would come, surprise had robbed him of what was left of his voice. Christos too, struggled to speak, his mind confused by the sound of his own familiar language.

'I am Esma,' she continued 'you will follow me.' She signalled to the oarswomen, who formed a guard around the men. 'You have done well.'

The four women clearly understood. Astonishing, considering that at no time in the days since the shipwreck did they manage any communication aside from eye contact and hand signals. Christos and Tomas had awoken in a state of delirium to find these women nursing them. The fact that the women must have understood every word spoken by the men sparked a flash of anger.

Esma sensed their reaction immediately and turned to face them, again holding up her hand sternly. Hot resentment deepened their bewilderment as they sputtered a few half formed questions. Esma simply stared them down, her eyes compelling them to patience. She turned back to the women

'What about Alphonse?'

The men were electrified, she knew about Alphonse!

'We left him sleeping,' replied one of the Sisters.

'But why!' cried Christos. 'Why leave him there?'

'His wounds have been tended. He has food, water and a palliative. He may be picked up by a passing boat.' Esma was finished with conversation, but Christos had thrown aside all caution.

'No boats come near here unless by freak of storm. Why could we not bring him with us?'

Esma ignored his question and indicated to the women that it was time to go. They set off two abreast along a steep track that led up the side of the rock, the track was well worn but shielded from view by a natural wall of granite. Weakened by their injuries, the men found it hard going and several rests were called for by their guards.

Within sight of an opening in the rock, they had to wait again for Tomas to regain his breath. Christos, although breathing hard, caught Esma's eye.

'Why?' he rasped.

Her penetrating stare stirred fear in the young man, but his gaze did not waver.

'Alphonse is beyond our help. His Fate is in his own hands,' she replied.

Stifling his rising alarm, and realising he was in no position to do or demand anything, Christos kept quiet.

Near the opening in the rock, two more white-robed older women emerged and stood aside for Esma and the nursing women to escort the men inside a cavern similar to the one on the islet. There were two beds made up on the floor of the cave, hot food simmered in a pot over a fire and there was a large clay pot of water.

'Make yourselves comfortable and we will check on you in the morning. We wish you a good night's rest.'

These last few words allayed doubt for the time. Christos and Tomas were both too tired to worry. It was enough to be alive and as far as they knew, safe.

CHAPTER TWO

Closer to the top of the rock, there was another opening, this one small and squat. All seven women stooped over to get through. Once on the other side, a large boulder was rolled into position to seal the entrance from inside. The entrance opened onto a naturally formed forecourt where the Sisters gathered each day to communicate with each other, for prayer, and for taking meals. Further inside the rock there was another area used for the same purpose when the weather was unkind.

There was no getting in or out of this entrance once the boulder was in place and the method of moving it ingeniously simple. The boulder was balanced on the edge of a rut. Two women could push it just enough for it to drop into a slightly deeper groove in front of the opening. Three or four women were required to lever it back into position. For the first time in the Sisters' history this night the entrance to their living quarters would be sealed.

Once inside, their silence was broken, and all started chattering at once. The four rescuers were to be feted for their bravery; it was always a risk to make the crossing to Luminetta and a greater risk to approach the men. The rescuers were delighted to be back and soaked up their welcome. Afterwards they hurried off to bathe and change into a fresh set of clothes. Very tired after their ordeal but buoyed by success they looked forward to the celebration their fellow Sisters prepared.

Reed torches lit the area. A simple meal of chicken and vegetables cooked in one pot was ready. A rooster had been sacrificed for the occasion and the rescuers guessed they would be given a good serve of meat as they had been living on cornmeal and fish for almost two weeks. Food was often in short supply on Luminos and their supply ship only came once every two years.

They called themselves the 'Sisters of Light', an ancient Society that had almost died out fifty years ago when a huge underwater earthquake lifted Luminos from the sea, splitting it from its outer crust of granite. When it all settled Luminos, enjoyed a higher elevation, but the granite 'crust' took up most of the small amount of arable land on the island and the entrance to their harbour was destroyed.

Most of the Sisters perished in that violent earthquake, only a dozen or so survived and they were determined to remain. For many years, Luminos had been a retreat for the small community of nuns who had set up in the abandoned St Catherine's Abbey on a most remote island, off the south-east coast of Greece, in the Aegean Sea. Over the years the numbers in their Luminos community fluctuated but they had still totalled about a dozen when Esma and five more females arrived in a large boat, about twelve years ago. Esma's group had been fleeing from cruelty and injustice, and at first had sought refuge at the Abbey. Esma had known of the retreat and hoped to be invited to stay there until she could formulate more permanent plans.

Sympathetic to the plight of Esma and her group, Eleanor, the Abbess of St Catherine's Abbey, was sorry to inform them that the harbour of Luminos had been partially destroyed many, many years ago and their boat was too big to be accommodated. Now it was necessary to off-load supplies at Luminetta and transport them via row-boat to Luminos. It was bitter news and a bitter disappointment for Esma's group. The *Raptor Queen* needed a secret and secure port, she was too noticeable to be left anywhere, and if seen word would soon get back to Alphonse.

At the time, Esma was worried that Alphonse might catch them. Would he guess she would make straight for the Abbey? She had tried to steer a confusing course, but couldn't waste much time because she expected him to be in hot pursuit. She was as sure as she could be that he had no knowledge of Luminos, but that was of no help if she couldn't use the place to secure her boat.

Back then Eleanor had suggested approaching Edward of Styne; who, with his Free Society of Stonemasons and Artisans, was presently engaged in a large restoration project in Asia Minor. He was known to charter boats, as he drew supplies from as far afield as China. More than once he had called on the Abbey to charter their boat when supplies were needed.

The two women had then settled down to discuss the problem, finally coming to an agreement. Esma would loan her boat to the Sisterhood for a period of two years renewable bi-annually, with free reign to charter the boat to Edward of Styne, with the proviso its name be changed to something more suited to their calling. This would be in exchange for the immediate transfer of the six refugees to the sanctuary of Luminos, via Luminetta, supplies delivered every two years and a return to the mainland for any of the women who wanted to go back.

In a speech at the 'Rescuers' dinner, Esma reminded all of the Sisters of their own individual journeys and the dangers they had faced.

'Now we have another problem,' she advised. 'I would like you to think about it ready for discussion tomorrow night.' She straightened her shoulders and looked around at the assembled diners. 'The older sailor is named Tomas and the younger one, Christos. They are both unknown to me. I am sorry to have to inform you that I have no doubt the one left to die on Luminetta; is my husband Alphonse.' She waited for the murmur of surprise to settle down.

'I always knew he would never forgive me for taking his boat and that he would track me down. I am not sorry for Alphonse or his predicament, but we do have to decide what to do with the other two. I leave the matter with you all to consider ready for discussion tomorrow.'

CHAPTER THREE

Later that night when all but Esma had retired, she received a request to join the 'Old Sisters' in their quarters. It wasn't unexpected. Esma knew they would want to know more about the current situation and only she was ever invited into their domain. Situated immediately above the inside forecourt there was a central open area where they sat and talked. Bordering this area were their individual cells, each decorated and made comfortable with rugs and cushions all hand-made from any fabric that could be re-cycled.

'Please sit down, Esma,' invited Helen, who was the most active of the old women and dutiful carer of Phoebe, the oldest and deeply revered leader of the last remnants of the true Sisters of Light. Phoebe seldom joined the community gatherings, finding talk exhausting. Her knowledge came from observation and contemplation, spending hours at her 'window' as she called it, a gap in the rock from which she could see Luminetta and the crossing. She also had a view of the path leading to the entry and the outer forecourt. Whisperings and laughter from the inner court, through some accident of acoustics, travelled along the contours of the rock and ended in the Old Sisters quarters. They knew everything without having to be seen or heard.

'We have reached a new stage of our journey together,' Helen began at a sign from Phoebe, when all were seated around in a circle of small benches carved from sandstone many ages ago. 'You and your friends came to us from the Abbey unexpectedly. It was at a time when we were nearing the end of our strength. We had striven hard in the years after the earthquake to put back together what we could of our home. We lay to rest our dead and lived among the ruins. The Abbey wanted us to leave Luminos, but we could not. Over the years the Abbey occasionally sent a party to check on our well-being. It wasn't a regular arrangement because at the time the Abbey did not have a boat. They would have had to charter one, which cost money and the Abbey is poor. Some of our Sisters returned when a boat came, especially if there was illness.' Helen cast a glance around the assembled women, age embraced them kindly, peace and contentment permeated the atmosphere. 'When your group arrived it boosted our morale. Suddenly life was easier, happiness returned and it seemed we had received a gift for all the years of struggle we had willingly endured.'

'Now there is another great change.' Helen looked directly at Esma. 'Our group of Sisters came to Luminos seeking solitude. Your group came seeking sanctuary. The years have done much to repair the lives of your women. We can sense there is an interest in the new arrivals. We would like to know if you had a premonition of this event and if you have a 'vision' of the future?'

'I feared Alphonse would track us down,' Esma admitted, speaking to all but looking directly at Phoebe. 'Taking his boat would have destroyed his prestige, opened him to ridicule and threatened his leadership. Opening the stopcocks of the only other boat in the fleet that could have given chase would have raised unimaginable fury. Because Alphonse's wife did this as well as taking his other wives and daughter, and the wife and daughter of the owner of the disabled boat, would add another dimension to his outrage. Wives are replaceable, but not so easily a boat! Alphonse would have been ruined.

There is a moral code among the islands but Alphonse ignored it because he is a formidable man. He influenced others to ignore it too. Once given time to reflect on the reasons for our flight, if those reasons are ever revealed, they would feel betrayed.

Alphonse's hatred for me drove him to rise again. I have felt safely out of his reach here on Luminos, but lately a 'coldness' has upset me. When it became obvious two of the shipwreck survivors were of a different caste we set about the rescue. When the nurse signalled Alphonse was there and badly injured, it was an easy decision to leave him behind. Loading an unconscious badly injured man onto the boat would have jeopardised the lives of all.

The two castaways we have saved may be of use to us. Christos is an attractive young man and not without courage. He will look for a means of escape. I think the older one will settle. I feel he has no family to draw him back to the mainland. While they are here they will be useful, I can think of much work they can do.'

Considering this information, the circle of old women was silent until Phoebe spoke so softly they all strained to hear.

'You must work this out, Esma. These are the tools you have been given to resolve the problems of your group and ours. This will be the final step for us all. I wish you goodnight.'

Phoebe raised her hand in a feeble gesture. Helen immediately came to her side and the Old Sisters arose as one to retire.

CHAPTER FOUR

The next morning Esma accompanied two of the nurses on their visit to Tomas and Christos. They found the men in happier spirits. A hot meal of meat and vegetables the previous night and a warmer bed to sleep in made them more relaxed about their predicament. They were ready to accept the rough boat trip across to Luminos could have killed Alphonse by cruelly aggravating his injuries.

It was obvious to Esma that Christos had been exploring. His hair was wet and so too the fragment of shirt he wore as well as his tattered trousers. He had been in the sea, but his feet were dirty. Dust from the path stuck to his wet skin.

'We have brought you something to wear,' she handed them each a bundle. 'There is a shirt for you to wear now and you must not appear among us without it. Soon the weather will be cold and you will need the other garments.' She peered narrowly at their ragged attire and noted they must be extremely hardy to have survived at all. 'We have also brought you some cornbread and fruit.' Esma looked pointedly at Christos's feet. 'Follow us now and we will show you where to wash and where to dispose of your rubbish. That's if you have not already found it yourself.'

Christos looked confused. He felt he had done the wrong thing and was uncomfortably sure that Esma knew that he had been up for hours checking out the surroundings. He had examined the boulder blocking the entrance to the Sisters' domain, hurried back to the harbour, diving in and swimming into the cavern to confirm that there were boats there. Then back to their cave where Tomas was still soundly sleeping.

Esma and the nurses led them down a side track to a fresh water pool. Climbing down the rocks, a little further below the pool was a rubbish disposal area which they noticed could also be a makeshift latrine where one had to sit over the edge of the rock, as one did over the side of a boat. The waves were only a few feet below, in bad weather they would have to choose their times carefully.

'I am sure you will be able to manage quite well,' Esma remarked, 'it is in keeping with life at sea for a sailor.' She turned around and indicated the vast blank slope of granite above them. 'This part of Luminos is the reason we can live here on the rock. That slope is our natural water supply. Rain hits the western face of the rock and runs down seeping through cracks, pooling in odd places throughout the rock itself. The ancients tapped into various pools and that is how we manage to water our gardens.'

'After you have cleaned yourselves up and dressed properly we will take you both down to where we work. You can help.' Esma looked at Tomas. 'Our fishing nets need some attention. It will be pleasant sitting in the sun mending them today. Do you think you can do that?'

Tomas was startled. He had hardly opened his mouth to speak since waking up on that little rocky beach when these silent robed figures were binding his wounds. He was grateful to them, but totally bewildered. At first he thought he had gone to heaven, but came to realise it wasn't so. Alphonse's moans put the lie to that fantasy. Christos' endless questions nearly drove him mad so he determined not to listen, to be thankful for the cornmeal and water and the gentle attention of the nurses. Gradually, he started to heal. Then there was the rough trip to this rock and then, last night, hot food and a good sleep.

'Yes, Ma'am,' he croaked, vocal cords stiff from disuse. 'I would be pleased to do a bit of fishing too, if you like, or any other job that needs doing.' His face was beet red from the effort, 'I am very grateful to you people for saving my life.'

'Thank you, Tomas,' Esma thought him a decent man.

Christos, however, could not meet her gaze. He felt she knew his thoughts. He decided to make a clean breast of it.

'I would like to thank you ladies too,' he began awkwardly. 'I would like to do what I can to help out. I went for a swim this morning and saw the boats in the dark cavern in the harbour and wondered if they are your fishing boats?'

'They belong to the Sisters of Light, the inhabitants of this rock – Luminos.' Esma saw from their faces they had no knowledge of the Sisterhood. 'There was an earthquake here many years ago and our home was ruined. Only a few of us survived.' Esma had no intention of revealing she and her followers were not of the Sisterhood. 'Those boats are trapped in the harbour and no longer seaworthy. Besides, they are far too large to make it out in one piece.'

With a promise to return later, Esma and the two nurses left the men to wash, dress properly, and take breakfast.

All had much to think about.

CHAPTER FIVE

By late morning, clad in the strong cotton shirt from the bundle of clothing supplied and his ragged trousers, Tomas sat on a rock with his back against the remains of an old seawall, working intently on a pile of netting. Giving his job total concentration, ignoring stiff fingers and aching back, he was making progress. It was good to be doing something. He didn't know where Christos had been taken, but felt sure his job would be harder. Christos seemed to have an uneasy manner with the Sisters, it was as if he had not fully realised that they had saved his life.

Tomas sat back for a moment, gazing around. The earthquake must have been enormous. He could see where it had made a cavern of the harbour, almost sealing it off, and he could see how the gigantic plates of granite had broken from the rock as it had been pushed upward. It was awe inspiring to contemplate. Luminos from East, South and West was impregnable. He shivered, wondering what lay to the North and whether he and Christos were truly marooned here in the middle of nowhere. So deep were his thoughts he did not hear the two women approach or the rattle of the small cart they were pulling along.

'Hello, you must be Tomas. We have brought you some lunch.' Jolted out of his imaginings, his facial expression was so comical the two women laughed, though not unkindly.

'Sorry to startle you. I am Doris,' said the nearest one, 'and this is Marla.' She spoke easily as she handed him a cup made from a gourd and began to pour him some water from a canvas bag. Tomas hastily scrambled to his feet to greet the women. They were both neatly made and of medium height, but Marla looked to be the strongest. She began filling a woven reed bowl with cornbread, slices of melon, and fried patties. As Doris filled the cup Tomas noticed her hands were neat and small and squarely shaped; practical hands that could work hard or bring comfort. Looking up at her he liked her face, not beautiful in the conventional sense, so he wondered why he found her so appealing. He drank thirstily and she refilled his cup. Both women were wearing the same type of shirt as had been provided for him, made in strong unbleached cotton, their ankle length trousers were of the same fabric and they wore hand- made canvas moccasins on their feet.

'Aren't you nuns?' Tomas couldn't help asking. The women had been briefed by

Esma on what information to give the men should the occasion arise.

'These are our working clothes. We wear our habits when work is done.' Marla informed him and forestalled further questions by handing him lunch. With his attention drawn to Marla, he thought he recognised her and being an honest man asked if she had been one of his rescuers.

'I'm not much of a nurse, but I can row a boat,' she replied, dismissing the subject. 'When you have finished the net I can help you set it out.' She looked at the pile of netting at his feet, 'Perhaps it will be ready the day after tomorrow? By the time it is ready to bring in we may have fish for the weekend.'

Having completely lost track of time, Tomas was surprised to discover that today must be Wednesday and there was a weekend to anticipate. Simple delight slowly registering on his face amused the girls afresh. 'We only work half a day on Saturday the rest of the day is ours to please ourselves,'

Marla explained. 'If you manage a good haul of fish, Esma may invite you to eat with us that night. If she does we will have to cut your hair and trim your beard otherwise you will frighten the Sisters to death,' she added mischievously.

Later that afternoon as the sky darkened toward early evening, Tomas stood up, stretched like a cat, tidied up the completed pile of mended netting and set off back up the path to his campsite. Stopping off at the pool, he washed vigorously enjoying the brisk chill of fresh water. He shook himself like a dog to remove most of the water, mopped himself dry with his old trousers and donning his shirt, ran quickly up the path to their cavern. Hunting through the clothing parcel he found a long sleeved vest and pair of panties to wear under a rough brown habit. Tomas dressed quickly. He felt reborn, clean, and at peace with the world. It was then he noticed the fire had been re-set and another pot of stew put in place. On closer inspection the stew looked to contain dumplings and tomatoes. It smelled delicious. Carefully, he lit the fire, fanning the flames until the tinder took hold.

Christos burst into their cavern, soaking wet, cold, tired and full of anger. Immediately, the fire started to splutter and smoke as Christos threw his arms about starting on a tirade of complaint about everything in general. Tomas firmly ushered him out of the cavern, there being no point in getting their living quarters damp.

'Calm down,' Tomas demanded. 'Why did you wash with your clothes on?' Tomas began stripping Christos and handed him his old clothes to mop himself up. It was obvious Christos had worked hard. He was still sweating despite being cold and wet.

'I've been back to the boats in the harbour, I wanted another look.' Tomas was amazed. To do that swim after a hard day's work cast doubt on how hard Christos had actually worked. He prompted Christos to explain.

Apparently, Christos had been put to work digging over compost all day. The Sisters were building beds from composted waste to grow food. They also had chickens in portable wire cages and Christos had been used to re-locate some of those cages. Tomas wondered from where they obtained the wire to build the cages and felt a twinge of excitement. There was much to learn about life on Luminos. Christos' greatest lament was he was expected to work like a serf. He was a seaman and didn't like digging in dirt. That was why he wanted another look at the boats, he was looking for escape.

Tomas felt a certain amount of pity for the young man as he handed him the vest, panties and habit from Christos' parcel and went about spreading out the sopping wet work clothes to dry.

'These are women's things,' Christos wailed, 'are they trying to turn us into women?'

'They are sharing with us what they have!' Tomas' voice was sharp. 'We are living with a company of nuns. You would do well to forget about your masculinity and show some respect!' The flash of temper from Tomas was a surprise to both men and set them thinking about their situation.

'They are probably keen to get rid of us,' Tomas mused, 'we are two more mouths to feed and an aggravation to their lifestyle! What is it you have in mind for the old boats?'

CHAPTER SIX

Christos was only too happy to explain what he had in mind for the old boats and Tomas listened patiently. It was obvious to the older man, the young fellow needed hope for escape or else he would do something dangerously reckless. Christos was thinking of making another boat from materials salvaged from the old wrecks. It had feasibility but many, many difficulties. Tomas waited until they had eaten their meal before he raised the problems they would face, but was careful not to be too negative.

'I think the Sisters would be very glad to be rid of us,' he began, 'so if we approach them reasonably they may be willing to help. We must bear in mind the wreckage is theirs and they may have some purpose for it. The other problem is that we would have to build a sturdy boat. No fragile raft could exit that harbour or even negotiate the reef, so it would have to be a good boat. That raises the question of whether or not they would want to hand it over to us when it was finished. All of this depends upon the availability of tools and other materials required for making a boat. It would take a very long time.' Tomas could see Christos becoming more and more deflated.

'You mentioned you saw chicken coops,' Tomas continued and Christos looked up in puzzlement. 'They must have obtained the wire for the coops from somewhere other than on this rock. I suggest we co-operate with the Sisters and try to find out how truly isolated we are, then we can assess our situation properly.' Christos visibly brightened.

Tomas continued, 'I have finished mending the nets so maybe tomorrow we will set them out. The one called Marla has offered to help me, but I will suggest you take my place and I do your job. That way you will be doing something you like while I will have a chance to take a look at the other end of the rock. What do you say?'

Christos readily agreed. Already he felt a stir of excitement.

Next morning, the two men were waiting outside their camp when the working party arrived led by Esma, who, although dressed in working clothes still maintained great dignity. It was a larger group than yesterday, seven women in all including Esma. Doris and Marla were present and Tomas noticed they were carrying the oars of the boat. He didn't fail to understand the oars were kept safely away from the boat overnight just in case the men made a dash for freedom. He looked at Esma and saw the ghost of an understanding smile. He could appreciate their caution; if positions were reversed he would do the same thing.

'You have done a good job with the nets Tomas. Marla and Thele will set them, Christos can row the boat. Once that is done, Christos can complete turning over the compost bed and then help us with our produce. We are harvesting some of our fruit today and taking it back to our storehouse.' Such was her penetrating gaze he felt she knew all his secrets. 'You may walk with me,' she said and he immediately obeyed.

'Where do you come from, Tomas?'

'Ambros,' he replied without hesitation, 'but I only have distant memories. I was orphaned at seven and taken in by an uncle who put me to work on his boat. I stuck it out until I was about twelve then took off. I have been drifting ever since.'

'And Christos?' Esma queried.

'He's not a drifter. He's part of the family who owns the boat we were on, the one that went down. They come from Yendruka. It's a great loss for him and his family which is why he is so anxious to get home.' They walked along in silence. Esma was relieved to discover the islands mentioned were far from Karakos and far from the Abbey too.

'Alphonse and I were picked up as last minute crew. Alphonse was desperate to be taken on and, if I had been chosen instead of him I think he would have done me in. A mystery to us all on board, he was dark tempered, kept to himself, but definitely on a mission. He asked us all if we had ever seen a particular boat and described it in detail. Only another seaman could understand such passion for a boat. It must have been seen in these waters for him to be so vitally interested in this particular voyage. He never stopped scanning the horizon.'

They reached the junction where the path, now with dirt mixed in with the sand

and shell-grit, veered away from the harbour and the fishing party separated from the gardening contingent.

'We have a boat bring us supplies every two years,' Esma continued their conversation as if there had been no interruption. 'It was here at the beginning of summer and won't be back for another twenty months. Sometimes it returns someone to the mainland, sometimes another person arrives seeking peace and solitude. That is when you and Christos can return to the Abbey at Xenos. If Christos can help us with a good supply of fish then he is welcome to salvage the old boats and try to build another one. We have a few tools he can use, but he will need to be a master boat builder to carry out his plan.'

Tomas was staggered that she knew of Christos's plan for the boats and Esma was quietly amused by the shock that registered on Tomas's face when he realised their plans were no secret.

'For a man of his background it would be the obvious thing to try to do,' Esma explained.

They walked along the path toward the gardens with Tomas lost for words, then another thought struck him. Could Alphonse's boat be the supply boat and what was the connection? He wondered. This was followed by a much more chilling thought, and he did not have the artifice to disguise the awareness written all over his face.

'You are thinking of Alphonse and questioning whether we deliberately left him to die?' Esma stated quietly, 'and the answer is exactly as you were told. He was too injured to survive the journey and would have put everyone else at risk.'

'Do you know if he has survived?'

'There has been no sign,' she replied and guided him towards the gardens.

Tomas was totally amazed at the variety and quantity of food produced. Not being of the land, he knew little of plants but did recognise melons, beans, tomatoes and many other food staples. He also saw an unusual building, difficult to describe because he could not see its purpose. Built of smallish rocks, it had a door of sorts, no windows and a flue at the top.

'That's our smokehouse,' Esma answered his unasked question. 'We depend on smoked fish for winter months. Luminos is bleak in winter the weather is rough, bordering on violent. If our stores are low, we must go hungry.

Luminos was no place for a holiday, Tomas decided as he recalled just how isolated and doomed they were. He found it astounding that these clever and resourceful women had chosen to live in this place. Surely they must have been beyond hope to seek solitude here.

'Where do you come from, Esma?' The question fell from his lips. It was no more than what she had asked of him, but he knew it to be presumptuous. He noticed her surprise but still waited for her answer.

CHAPTER SEVEN

'I come from the Abbey,' she replied, 'all of us do. We came seeking solitude and contemplation, surviving is a test of our faith and resolve.'

Tomas didn't know how to answer, so he said nothing, just nodded as if he understood. It was incomprehensible to him that women should want to live in such a place and now he was even more convinced there was a much bigger reason for their presence.

Esma walked with him to the orchard section where he was introduced to Kaliope and Ana. Tomas hadn't ever met such elderly ladies. They were small, gentle, softly spoken and very pretty in a frail way. They suited the green leafy part of the garden where they worked, their white hair and pink cheeks reminded him of some blossom he had seen long ago. They showed him what fruit to pick, the method of picking it so as not to damage the tree or the product, and to place it in a basket and then put the filled basket into a cart. For Tomas, who had never worked on the land before, it was a Utopian experience. He filled twice as many baskets as they did and when the cart was full, offered to push it back to where it was to be delivered.

'You can't go there without us,' they explained so Tomas suggested they come along for the ride. There was room for the women to stand in the cart and hold onto the sides for support, so with childlike excitement, the two ladies climbed on board. It was hard work when they got to the uphill part of the pathway but Tomas didn't mind, he was glad to note his strength was returning and they laughed and gasped so much all the way up to the entrance of their living quarters, it was well worth the effort. Helen was waiting just outside the opening of the rock and stood aside while Tomas helped the two passengers out of the cart.

'We have had such fun,' they chimed, 'and Tomas filled our cart so quickly.'

Helen signalled to someone the other side of the entrance to pull the cart through and while this was happening handed them each a cup of water.

'Are you going back?' he asked.

'I want to go back,' Kaliope ventured, 'there is still more fruit to pick before the light fades but mostly I would like a ride down-hill.' Their excitement at such simple pleasure touched Tomas. His experience with women was very limited and he had never known 'ladies of the cloth' as he described them to Christos. Their innocence refreshed him and he could feel a strengthening power in his body and soul.

Christos' day too was rewarding. A reasonable catch provided enough food for a good meal that night and there were hopes of improvement.

'I can better place the nets,' he explained to Tomas as they sat at their fire each grilling a fish on a stick, 'but I have to convince the girls.'

Marla and Thele found no difficulty in accepting advice from a fisherman and gladly followed Christos' advice with good results. The improvement continued each day so that it became necessary to stoke up the smoke-house. Tomas was called upon to help with scaling, gutting and threading the fish onto sticks to place in the racks of the smoke-house. Seagulls appeared from nowhere raucously swooping on discarded fish gut and fearlessly snatching a fish as often as possible. No-one minded sharing a few with the birds; they too fought hard to survive.

This busy, noisy productive period continued for several weeks, only relieved by Saturday afternoons, when the men were able to spend time preparing the old boats in the cavern for hauling ashore.

A boat had to be lightened as much as possible by removing any un-necessary top structure so that it would rise higher in the water allowing for more water to be bailed out, thus lightening it further. It was a tedious process but of vital interest to the two men. They were on the cusp of bringing in their first boat when they received an invitation to take an evening meal with the Sisters.

They were hesitant to accept, but Doris and Marla had also arrived with hair grooming and shaving equipment and said there was no avoiding it. They also brought each man a gift of a pair of canvas moccasins made by the old Sisters.

The men reluctantly submitted to the barbering and then spent some time airing and brushing their habits, which they had been using as sleepwear. By the time they were thoroughly bathed, it was time to go.

'Make sure you wear your undergarments,' Tomas warned Christos who still rebelled against wearing ladies panties. 'It would be a pity to accidentally upset the Sisters after all this effort'.

Looking ethereal in their white habits the Sisters of Light were assembled ready to greet their guests. Waiting at the entry, Esma led the men forward to meet Sister Superior.

Phoebe had not come face to face with either of the men before and keen interest brightened her almost black eyes. She was very small, but had enormous presence.

Tomas had never seen such eyes; they were as dark as moonless midnight. Although being aware of the introduction and other Sisters standing around, his total focus was on Phoebe whose gaze held him in her grip. She was reading his soul and now he had a feeling that she knew everything possible to know about him. Surprisingly, she offered her hand. He raised it to his lips, but with ultimate respect, did not touch it just bowed his head.

'You are very welcome to be among us, Tomas.' Choked by sudden emotion he could only nod in response.

Distinctly underwhelmed when introduced to the Old Sisters, Christos could not understand Tomas' connection with them. Nor was he interested, just glad Marla and Thele were his main contacts in this strange place. It came as a delightful surprise to find they each had a daughter and both were absolutely gorgeous. Milla, the elder of the two resembled her mother Marla, dark and luscious. Bebe, still a teenager, was quiet like Thele with little to say, but light in colour and manner and as innocently curious as a kitten.

Cups of wine were handed around. Another unexpected surprise!

'We make it ourselves mostly from the plum crop,' Esma explained, 'make sure you take it carefully.'

'An unnecessary warning,' Christos wryly commented to Tomas later as they were not offered a second cup. Free to sit where-ever they wished, Tomas chose to sit beside Doris. Christos placed himself between the two young girls, both men acutely aware nothing they said or did would go un-noticed by the Sisters.

The men had not attended a large dinner in years. In this instance Christos was more at ease because it resembled a family gathering. Tomas had no memory of a celebration to draw on so he settled down to enjoy whatever unfolded. The dinner was a simple delight. Lightly herbed vegetable soup started the meal, followed by fish pie. The Sisters used very small fish and baked them in a tart with their heads and tails sticking up through the pastry. Tomas had never seen anything like it before and thought it the best food he had ever tasted. That was until he tasted the whole un-peeled roasted peach, served in its own caramelised juice and topped with almond paste. He was so impressed he asked Doris how it was made.

'We blanche the almonds, then grind them to a paste using a mortar and pestle,' she explained to Tomas, who was still none the wiser.

Their undisguised enjoyment of the food pleased the Sisters as well as the good manners displayed. An evening intended to get to know the men better had served its purpose. After thanking their hostesses and taking their leave, they were the general subject of discussion. As yet it was unclear to the Sisters what purpose these men would serve but their faith told them there was one. They did not believe in random accident.

Phoebe retired, indicating to Helen she would rest by her window this night. Helen realised immediately Phoebe had something on her mind. Helen wasn't surprised the next morning when she brought in her morning cup of tea to find Phoebe dressed and asking for Esma to be brought 'as soon as possible.' Helen hurried off hastily.

Phoebe was standing upright when Esma arrived. She looked stronger than at any time in all of their acquaintance.

'Alphonse lives,' she announced, 'and will be here once he has found a way.'

A shiver passed over Esma.

'The evil power that drives him has put Alphonse on our doorstep. It is inconceivable he has survived. I deeply regret placing you and the Sisters in danger. Do not doubt I will deal with him!'

'We will deal with him together, Esma! Helen and I will keep watch from my window and you will be told of any movement!'

Incredibly touched, Esma hurried away, she needed to be alone. Alphonse should have died, hatred kept him alive. She should have provided a stronger palliative, but then she argued that would not have been 'right'.

She should have instructed the nurses not to leave the palliative, but that wouldn't have been 'right' either. She should have known that as soon as he saw the phial he would know she was near and that had given him the will to survive.

She had to face the consequences of her actions taken so long ago.

CHAPTER EIGHT

Luminetta stood outside the reef at the south-eastern end of Luminos surrounded by a tumble of rocks, some big some small. No foliage softened the landscape but there was debris from other plant life that arrived storm-tossed from the swirls of surrounding currents. Snared by the sharp teeth of some rocks and imprisoned by the bulk of others, it provided sustenance for life-forms that in turn provided nourishment for other small marine creatures.

Aware of none of this, Alphonse began to stir from his coma. Awakening in the dark of the night, registering only the familiar smell of sand and ocean, but feeling warm and dry he immediately returned to sleep. The next time he stirred there was light, but sleep overpowered him again. Finally, when he did regain consciousness, a raging thirst forced him to raise his head and try to focus on his surroundings. Dim light showed them as bleak and comfortless. There was no sound other than the rhythmic thump and sigh of the ocean.

Slowly adjusting to the gloom, he could see a cup on a nearby bench. Reaching for it brought unexpected pain. Nearly fainting, he lay still. He was wounded. It took some time for him to work out which movements caused least discomfort. Fingers of daylight crept into the cavern long before he managed to inch close enough to the bench to grasp the cup. Thankfully it contained water and he drank greedily. Falling back on his bed, he understood he must have been placed here. But who could it have been? And where were they now?

Memories of the storm came back. Horrendous noise! Jagged lightning! Flashes of murderous seas! Black waves like monsters rising high and crashing down with lethal intent. Blacker skies smothered the moon and the stars were gone. There was no way of knowing which way was up. It was unleashed madness, screaming wind and the cracking, splintering screech of their boat as it succumbed, swallowed alive by a voracious ocean. And then... oblivion!

The needs of his body brought him slowly back from darkness. Thirst, forced him to reach for more water. He then tried to eat the cornmeal dry, but choked, so mixed it with the water and it quelled his hunger for a time. Shaking from the effort of feeding himself, he looked down at his own body and saw the whitish pap of spilled cornmeal stark against his blackened skin. He hadn't noticed before, but he was profoundly bruised and lacerated. Bandages had been applied to some wounds; abrasions had been painted with healing ointment.

Something stronger than pain tore through his consciousness. Ignoring distress, he rolled from his bed onto his knees, peering closely at the items on the low bench alongside his sleeping place. Pushing aside the cup and bowl, he reached further into the shadows at the back of the bench and withdrew a medicine phial that looked familiar. Sinking back on his heels he clutched the bottle and let out a strangled howl of raw hatred. Esma was near. He shook with triumph. Twelve years of searching and she was close. More witch than woman, he knew she had saved his life, only to let him die. He tasted the contents of the phial carefully and experienced the glorious relief the medicine brought and knew that was the torment. Relief would be fleeting, temptation to drink more or all of the contents would be terrible, if he did he would die. He knew Esma and credited her with great cunning. After all, it was all he knew, and could not conceive she had any other purpose than to torment and destroy him.

He allowed himself a sip at dawn and at dusk. In between those times he slept, drank water and ate cornmeal. Ignoring the pain, he tried moving his limbs and body very carefully, grimly persisting until, after several days he could crawl. Setting small targets, he made his way agonisingly slowly to the mouth of the cavern where he sat trying to take in his surroundings. Tall and imposing, Luminos (although he did not know its name) glowered down on Luminetta, where he was (he did not know this rock's name either) but felt convinced he was prisoner under scrutiny. Reinvigorated by fresh air and sunshine he noticed the black bruises were now dark purple with tinges of red and took heart in the improvement. He then shrewdly began plotting his next move.

First, he needed more food. As if on cue, a small sand crab scuttled past. He snatched it up, smashed it against a rock, and ate it raw, sucking every last drop of flesh and juice out of the shell. The best place to find food would be nearer the shore but, looking up at Luminos, he decided someone could be watching at this moment. Determined to destroy Esma, but not before discovering what she had done with his boat, his recovery would have to be secret. He wriggled back into the mouth of the cavern. A little beach not far from the cavern would be ideal to bathe his wounds in seawater and there was the prospect of food but he could only visit in the hours of darkness. Back inside the cavern it smelled unpleasantly stale but he was glad to reach his bed to rest and make plans.

A few weeks later, he could move more easily and had found a way to the back of his rock (as he described Luminetta) out of the sight of her rock, (which was the name he gave Luminos). Before dawn each day, under the cover of his blanket he painfully escaped the cavern and crept to the off-side of the rock where he spent the day feeding, bathing and basking in the sun. During these weeks, he stripped the rocks of their colony of periwinkles and molluscs, consumed dozens of crabs and ate raw fish.

He never forgot to be cautious but one day the raucous cries of seabirds in a feeding frenzy drifted across the water from Luminos. It aroused his curiosity and using his bed rug, which was now a very dirty grey, as cover, he hid underneath it and took up a position where he could spy on the big rock. A few hours later he observed wisps of smoke rising into the air. It was the first indication of life he had seen. A need for action stirred and he knew he was ready to complete his mission.

Crossing the ocean between the two rocks, passing through the reef and getting onto the rock seemed impossible, but there must be a way. The distance wasn't beyond him but lack of knowledge of the surrounding sea posed a great risk. Alphonse decided to study the ocean huddled under his rug. He would be in full view of the big rock but difficult to see in daylight and almost impossible to detect in the dark.

One night when the moon was full he saw the light. It was a narrow gleam of light shining on the surface of the ocean, disappearing and then re-appearing with the movement of the water. It passed through the reef and ended near the base of the rock. He watched it for a long time coming to the conclusion it indicated a channel. He had only heard of such a phenomenon.

There was no doubt in his mind this was his chance, and he was ready. Grimly determined he took off the rug and waded into the sea.

CHAPTER NINE

On the day of the first full moon after harvesting, a special dinner was held in celebration. Tomas and Christos were invited to attend. Some weeks had passed since their first invitation to dine with the Sisters, so they were looking forward to the occasion. For Christos it meant something special to eat and another cup of wine as well as being able to talk about his boat plans. Salvaging a boat by partially dismantling it, bailing out as much water as possible by hand because they had no pump, and beaching what remained of the wreck before taking that apart, was extremely hard work.

'We couldn't have got this far alone,' Christos was proud of their achievement but wanted to acknowledge the Sisters' help. 'I would like to say a few words of thanks, but am afraid of offending by speaking at their 'Moon Festival.' What should I do?'

'Ask Marla,' Tomas advised, 'and at the same time find out if she will trim our hair. We need to look as tidy as possible.' Not having seen Doris since the last dinner, Tomas wondered if he was being avoided and was becoming obsessed with her.

'She is in the group that 'put down' our harvest,' Marla explained during his hair-cut. Somewhat relieved, he accepted that reason, but still wondered why she had not come down with some of the other Sisters on Saturdays, to see the progress they were making on wrecking the old boats. Bemused by Tomas' manner and the extraordinary length of time he spent grooming for the occasion, Christos copied to the extent of presenting himself neatly too. Marla also arranged for Christos to speak during the 'Acknowledgement of Blessings'.

On the night, Esma welcomed them, and Phoebe, who was seated, nodded in their direction her eyes seemingly blacker than ever. She openly appraised them, extending her hand first to Tomas and then Christos. In turn they each bowed low over her hand without kissing it and there was an extraordinary intensity between all three. Tomas could feel her power. Christos felt bewildered by her manner, her voice and the scrutiny they received.

'I am very glad you are here.' Those were her words but so hard to distinguish the men couldn't be sure.

Tomas was in popular demand with the Sisters but it was easy to see his mind was elsewhere. It was clear the moment Doris approached. They all observed with avid interest the flush that tinged his cheeks when she greeted him, and his awkward, stumbling reply.

'I thought you might be avoiding me and worried I had offended you in some way.' Openly eavesdropping, the Sisters pressed a little closer.

'I have taken vows Tomas and must be careful of friendship with gentlemen.' Doris spoke so sweetly the Sisters sighed for Tomas who had been gently put in his place. 'That is not to say you may not sit beside me at dinner tonight and I am very curious to learn of your plans and how they are progressing.'

Tension partially relieved, their friendship was able to resume and they took up their seats alongside Christos, Marla and Milla. Bebe was to waitress for the night. Eggnog, made from almond milk, eggs and their own distilled spirit was being served. Tomas found the drink too rich for his taste, but for Christos it was a reminder of home, he loved it and said as much.

'You have mine, Christos, I'll stick with water.' Tomas pushed his cup over to his friend.

Celebrations commenced with an acknowledgement of their blessings. It turned out to be a long list, which the men thought to be an exaggeration considering how hard they all worked. To the un-initiated, the Moon Celebration was a boring occasion, however, Christos made his little speech which pleased the Sisters, and dinner did not disappoint. Afterwards, there was some singing and prayers that their blessings continue. Young Bebe who, thinking she was giving Christos a treat, refilled both empty cups with more eggnog. Tomas noticed and a short time later rose to his feet to say 'goodnight' to his hostesses.

'I think it is time for us to go, my young friend has had a very busy day.' As Christos made no complaint, they all accepted that reason for the men leaving early but it was Tomas who really wanted to make his escape.

Feeling bitterly let-down and depressed by Doris's rebuff, he realized how much he had been looking forward to resuming their acquaintance, Christos fell onto his bed fully clothed and fell asleep instantly.

Tomas laid down on his own bed his mind buzzing with questions. Why were there two groups of Sisters? Why was there such a big age gap between the groups? Why did two of the younger Sisters each have a daughter? Where was this Abbey from which they came? Why did Doris remind him she had taken a vow? Could she have feelings for him?

The last question disturbed him most, bringing him to his feet to pace back and forth before the surprising truth brought him to a halt. It was a staggering realisation. He had always felt worthless. When he was orphaned, his uncle took him in reluctantly, putting him to work on his boat, probably because his aunt didn't want him in their home. His aunt treated him as an intruder in their family. Ashamed of his dependence, he ran away when he was twelve years old. He found work on other boats and was big and savvy enough to avoid trouble, but having no home reinforced his sense of worthlessness. Being shipwrecked and saved by the Sisters changed his life. He found grace and respect among them and a return of self-esteem. They renewed him. All his adult life he yearned for family but did not expect fulfilment. Meeting Doris revived that wish. Something about her touch brought back long forgotten memories. Too distant to clearly recall, they teased him with a promise of sweetness and care. He watched and waited for her each day, more and more intensely.

Too restless to be confined inside their cave, he emerged into the night breathing deeply in an effort to calm his nerves and noticed movement along the path to the harbour. It was Esma, and something about her manner stopped him from calling out.

Staring straight ahead, pace slow but steady, arms folded across her waist and hands hidden in the sleeves of her habit, she appeared to be in a trance. He watched for a few minutes then saw she was being followed by another Sister, this one moving unsteadily, even more slowly and was supported by a sturdy walking stick. He was absolutely amazed to recognise Phoebe. Too curious to let the matter lie, he moved silently keeping to the shadows and followed.

CHAPTER TEN

The full moon clearly illuminated the pathway, intensifying shadows along the edge. Tomas kept to them, not wanting to be seen. He was alarmed by Esma's and Phoebe's manner of movement and his own instinct warned him of danger.

Not altering her gait, Esma continued to the small pier almost stiffly, mounted the few stone steps, proceeded to the middle, and stopped. She stared into the black mouth of the cavern and waited. Phoebe reached the steps, shakily climbed them, and sat on a bollard at the corner of the pier. Neither woman spoke to the other.

'I know you are there Alphonse! Come out and say what you must!' Esma sounded strong and purposeful.

Tomas was stunned. Alphonse alive! Here! Tomas assumed him dead, though instantly felt ashamed that in the selfish need to survive, willingly accepted all he had been told. He and Christos seldom mentioned Alphonse's fate. It was difficult to confront the fact that someone had been left to die, but the circumstances were extraordinary, and he believed the Sisters had no other choice.

'Where is my boat?' a gravelly voice, harsh with anger and undisguised hatred, broke into Tomas' thoughts and he was startled by the appearance of a large, gaunt, hairy man at the end of the pier who was unmistakably Alphonse.

'It is no longer in my keep. I traded it for sanctuary in this place.' Esma firmly stated.

A howl of rage went up. 'Who has it now?' He took a step threateningly toward her and Tomas saw Phoebe take up her stick as a weapon instead of a prop and move toward Esma.

'The Sisterhood,' Esma replied. Another howl rent the dark night. He loathed the Sisterhood. He loathed Esma and her father who had supported his daughter and the lunatics who made up the Society of the Sisters of Light.

'Then where is it?' Alphonse could barely keep himself in check. He was expecting to find the boat here in some concealed waterway and was angry and confused it was not to be seen. Since surviving the perilous crossing from the little island, he had only found gardens and a smoke house plus the wreckage of some boats. There must be a cove on the other side of the rock.

'It is not here!' Sounding cold and distant, Esma could not have goaded him more.

'Liar!' he screamed and, moving faster than anyone could expect, he crossed the few feet between them and lunged for her throat, grabbing it with both hands. Trying to pull his hands away she dropped her dagger. Phoebe moved with unexpected speed and began attacking Alphonse with her walking stick. Still clutching Esma's throat with one hand he wrenched the stick from the old woman and brought it down heavily across her head and shoulder.

Racing across the pathway as soon as he saw Phoebe go to Esma's aid, Tomas saw her brave attack and the savage blow that brought her down. Seeing Phoebe lay unmoving and Esma on her knees half strangled, a mighty roar erupted from his lungs. They were his people.

The strength of ten men flooded his veins and everything went red as he launched himself at Alphonse. Several savage blows across his face were unfelt before he got close enough to wrestle the stick from Alphonse. Phoebe still lay at their feet. Alphonse had the strength of a madman, but so too did Tomas. Released, Esma fell to the ground while the two men fought, exchanging heavy blows.

Loudly gasping for breath and almost insensible Esma tried to stand but was knocked down by the struggling men. Her hand fell upon the dagger. Picking it up, she began feebly stabbing at Alphonse's bare feet.

Viciously kicking out, Alphonse lost balance, falling heavily and bringing Tomas down too. Tomas struggled to his feet, but Alphonse did not move.

Suddenly, there was silence. The only sound was that of rough breathing and the drumming of heartbeats.

'Oh, dear God, what has happened?' Helen burst upon the scene, barely being able to take in the details. Phoebe was her first concern; she knelt alongside her feeling for a pulse. There was a faint one and she looked around for clarification. Unable to speak Esma, motioned to Tomas.

'The two Sisters were attacked by this man,' Tomas began just as Marla, Thele and Doris arrived. 'I think he is dead.'

Suddenly, there seemed to be people everywhere.

'Get the stretcher,' Marla ordered, 'and Christos,' she added, knowing his strength would come in handy.

The stretcher was speedily produced and Phoebe carefully and lovingly carried to their sanctuary. Esma, although tall was quite light so Christos was able to pick her up easily enough and carry her back to the Sisters' quarters, manoeuvring her carefully through the low entry with admirable strength and dexterity. For the moment, Alphonse was forgotten.

'Light the fire!' someone shouted, 'and the torches!' There was a flurry of activity. 'Make two beds!' Helen was giving orders like a general almost running Christos off his feet, shifting tables and benches, hefting mattresses, drawing water to boil.

'Check up on Tomas, Doris,' she ordered, 'I think he is hurt! And take some blankets to cover the body. We will examine the scene when it is light. Bring Tomas back here, he is wounded and will need attention.'

Sitting on the bollard where Phoebe sat earlier, staring into space, Tomas' thoughts were chaotic. With so many questions churning around in his mind, he didn't hear Doris approach. But her gentle touch erased all emotional turmoil, calming and easing his spirit.

'Oh! My dear Tomas, what has he done to you?' cupping his face gently in her hands, and lightly kissing his brow. Tomas knew he would go through a thousand beatings to hear those words again. He gazed at her, mutely adoring.

'We need to talk, but first we must attend to your poor dear face.'

Doris handed the blankets to two of the Sisters who followed her down to the pier. They would cover the body, secure the scene and possibly stay on guard until daybreak. It was a relief to see them. Doris didn't want to look at or touch Alphonse's body.

'Lean on me,' she invited Tomas. He didn't need to, his strength had returned the moment he saw her, but he couldn't resist putting his arm around her as they made their back to the Sister's sanctuary.

CHAPTER ELEVEN

'It's Tomas!' the word buzzed around and immediately he was beset by his elderly admirers who tenderly cared for his cuts and bruises whilst anxiously probing about his assailant.

'Luminos killed him,' Tomas replied, tiredly honest. 'All three of us were no match for that man. He was insane. He lost his footing, fell, taking me down with him and hit his head on the kerbstone. I heard the soft 'crack' of his bone. I felt a slight tremor in his body, I heard a gasp and he was still.' There was quiet while they absorbed this news. 'Tell me about Phoebe,' his voice was husky and distressed.

'All is not well,' Kaliope informed him. 'Her shoulder is broken and probably smaller bones besides. She is too fragile to move and we won't leave her side. 'Esma's throat is too damaged to speak. She is badly shaken, but will recover.'

Tomas gazed around. This place, which only hours ago had been the happy scene of their Moon Festival, now resembled a field hospital. Accepting an offered drink gratefully, he found it warm, spicy and incredibly soothing. He knew it would put him to sleep, and that was what he needed to restore his strength. Something told him this was only the beginning - of what, he did not know, but something was building. He could feel it.

Christos was sitting looking at him when Tomas awoke.

'Ah, you're awake at last!' Christos grinned cheekily. 'Trust you to get all the glory and me all the work. Things have been happening.' He set down a mug of herbal tea, some cornbread and soft fruit. 'Once you have eaten, the Sisters want to 'interview' you then later on today we will have a burial for Alphonse. They have been busy since sunrise, inspecting the scene in fine detail and then the body before preparing it for burial. Have you ever lifted a dead body? I never imagined it would be so heavy!' Christos didn't wait for an answer. 'Anyway it is now wrapped in that canvas I managed to salvage from the old boat and he will be buried at sea later today. They expect us to attend, probably to shift the body around.'

Christos chattered away excitedly. He too, could feel change in the air. 'I think I know how Alphonse got here! 'Do you remember when we were brought across to this Rock? How the Sisters watched the ocean for ages before they suddenly decided to shove off! I think Alphonse must have seen that sign too. He was a good seaman and a strong swimmer. The fact he survived at all amazes me. I know they gave him up for dead, but I wonder why they didn't check him out to make sure! He must have had a good snoop around while we were at dinner. He found the smoke-house; there are the remains of a few fish, so he must have been hungry.'

The Recorders of the Sect interrupted to interview Tomas and they took infinite care to understand every nuance of his description of what had occurred. Christos listened in to every word, and wished that he had been there too. He realised he loved the Sisters and would gladly have defended them.

'Why didn't you wake me?' he asked Tomas as soon as they were alone.

'I wish I had! I felt uneasy when I saw them go by, that is why I followed. I thought it may have been a private part of the 'Moon Ritual' and if it was I would have returned. I never expected to see Alphonse.'

The Sisterhood gathered at the pier at sundown.

'Why are the Old Sisters doing everything?' Christos asked Tomas, who shrugged his shoulders and offered a wry expression. It hurt to make a face, so it was a very fleeting grimace almost unnoticeable under the blackened bruises and swollen eyes. He could not see very well at all.

'Who is here?' Tomas wanted to know if Doris was around but didn't want to show his interest too plainly. Christos scanned the crowd.

'Helen is in charge, she is standing on the pier steps. The Old Sisters are gathered in front of her on the path, the younger ones are standing behind them, and Esma is right at the back. She looks terrible. Her throat is black and her hair seems to be whiter and standing straight up. She would scare anyone. Doris, Marla and Thele are with her but I can't see the young girls. I remember someone saying they were to be on hand for the nurse who is caring for Phoebe, should she need help.'

The ceremony began with prayers for the stranger who had come among them. Helen mentioned his courage and endurance, leaving it to God to judge the purpose of his actions.

The two men were summoned to carry the stretcher bearing the body to a place a small distance from the pier where the wall of rock dipped to about shoulder height. There was an opening just wide enough to take the width of the stretcher. They manoeuvred themselves into place, one each side of the stretcher, lifting it to knee height, then changing their grip to hoist it over head to rest the foot end on the opening. Tomas took the weight for a few seconds while Christos, who was tallest, switched to the head of the stretcher and raised it as high as possible. Tomas moved underneath to help push the litter upwards and forward, then together they slowly raised the angle until they felt the body start to slip. A few more good pushes and Alphonse's body began to slide smoothly, then rapidly, until the weight was gone and the men dropped the stretcher and clambered up the rock to peer over the edge in time to see the body splash into the sea and disappear.

'I'm glad that's over,' Christos muttered and received a cautionary nudge from Tomas. The two men were almost exhausted, but stood quietly while Helen closed the service.

Trudging back up the path towards the Sanctuary they were surprised to hear agitated voices up ahead. It was Bebe.

'Come quickly! Oh, please, come quickly!'

CHAPTER TWELVE

Tomas and Christos were first to arrive back at the Sanctuary but were brushed aside by Esma and Helen.

It was the usual practice for illness or injury to be treated in the communal areas of the Rock because of better light and easier access to the patient. It could also be added that fresh air too, was of great benefit. Privacy screens were erected when inside, outside a small tent was used.

However, Phoebe had wanted to watch the burial proceedings from the 'window' in her cell and, although there were doubts about moving her at all, without uttering a word she made it clear that she was compelled to see the burial of her assailant.

The two women hurried into the inner sanctum, leaving the men feeling useless.

'Let's take a cart each and bring some of the older Sisters back from the pier', Tomas suggested, 'they have had enough excitement in the last twenty-four hours!' Christos agreed and soon they were offering rides and the Sisters were most relieved and grateful.

Phoebe appeared to be sleeping as the two women quietly approached the bed, Helen giving precedence to Esma who was considered a doctor. The patient, without opening her eyes, drew them closer. She wanted to communicate and she wanted them to listen.

'I saw Esma's husband on Luminetta and knew he would come for her. My assistance was useless but Luminos prevailed. It was a rapturous relief.' She appeared to sleep for a few minutes but Esma and Helen stayed still. 'The moment his body was returned to the sea our two young girls, Milla and Bebe appeared by my bed.' Phoebe opened her eyes and there was radiance in her gaze.

'They could have been my sister and I when we were young, one dark one fair. That wonderful feeling returned.' Phoebe attempted a smile, 'I feel forgiven. I am free to go.' Tears were running down Esma's cheeks, so too Helen's. 'I want you both to hear my confession.'

Her words were hardly a breath yet they sounded clearly in their ears. They looked at each other in astonishment. 'We hear you,' was all they could think of to say.

'I committed a great sin many, many years ago!' There was a long pause, but no-one made a move or a sound.

'My sister and I had travelled to the new land to bring the Sisterhood to that place.' Once again there was a long pause and absolutely no movement from Phoebe.

'We were successful and made a powerful friend. My sister fell in love with that friend.'

This time the pause was so lengthy Esma and Helen were tempted to move but managed to stay fast.

'She became 'with child', there was a great scandal, and we had to leave the city and go into hiding. My sister died while giving birth and I was left with a baby girl.' This time there was no temptation to break the silence or to move, they just waited for as long as it took for Phoebe to finish her story.

'I buried my sister in a lonely place by the sea, left the child on the steps of an orphanage, and took passage on a trading ship back to the Abbey.' Phoebe looked deathly pale but she had not finished.

'The Sisterhood's Sanctuary on Luminos had been almost destroyed by earthquake, so I volunteered to re-establish the Sanctuary as penance for my sins. It took me a long while to acknowledge my guilt in my sister's affair. Her lover gave us free accommodation and showered us with gifts, I should not have allowed that to happen. I should have kept the baby, but I left it to its fate.' The old lady held out both hands, they were no more than claws. The two women each took one, stroking it gently.

'You both must take the Sisterhood back to the mainland. You will know what to do when the time comes. I wish to be burnt on the pyre at the top of Luminos. I will be part of the light to bring the ship here and will be the last to die on this Rock!'

Esma and Helen sat holding her hands, not realising for a few moments that she was gone. They gazed at each other and suddenly grief broke. Their sobs were dry and harsh and unbelieving. To them Phoebe was immortal. They couldn't imagine life without the one who was so small, so quiet, and yet who wielded such power.

Not having the strength just yet to tell the others, they sat quietly contemplating the future.

When they did emerge, there was no need for words, their body language said all that was necessary. Most of the Sisters fell to their knees to pray, others stood about bewildered.

Tomas and Christos saw the emotional disarray and tactfully withdrew.

'The news must be the worst,' Christos commented, returning to their camp. He looked at Tomas and saw that he too looked beaten and depressed.

'I admired Phoebe,' Tomas confessed, 'She attacked Alphonse like a lioness defending her cubs.' A tear rolled down his swollen, bruised face.

'It has been a hard day,' Christos said, surprised at the emotion shown, and impressed with the older man's manner. Not once had Tomas complained about their situation, he just got on with the job of surviving, doing what was necessary and along the way had formed a bond with the Sisters.

'Take a rest! You look like you need it!' Christos said, 'I set a line earlier today I'll go

see if I've caught something for our supper.
We will feel better after something to eat.'

Touched by Christos's unexpected
compassion, Tomas gratefully sank down on
his own bed, while Christos hurried off to the
little beach.

CHAPTER THIRTEEN

Around mid-morning the next day, the Sisters represented by Doris and a nurse, made contact with Tomas and Christos. They found them at their wrecking site re-stacking wood.

'We have come to confirm what you must already know,' Doris gently informed them, 'Phoebe has passed on.' A solemn quietness enveloped all four for a few moments. 'We have also come to dress your wounds, Tomas, and then ask you both to join us in our sanctuary for a meeting.' While speaking, Doris peered closely at Tomas's face, the bruising was coming out which made him appear more blackened and puffy.

'Will you bury Phoebe at sea?' Christos asked curiously. It had bothered him most of the night. It felt wrong to bury her as they did Alphonse, which was not far away from where they tipped their waste into the ocean. But little ground around here could be spared for a grave. Christos had explored all of the area of the Rock he could access and never saw a grave or a memorial and wondered if there was a crypt inside the Rock.

'Phoebe's burial and service will be discussed when you join us.' Doris wasn't exactly short with Christos but her tone ended his questioning. In the meantime, Tomas sat placidly having his wounds treated, just happy to be near Doris who was interested in the nurse's work and raised a query from time to time.

Soon they were all at the sanctuary where the Sisters had gathered in the outside community area. Everyone looked tired.

Overnight, Esma and Helen had been interviewed by the Recording Sisters who also interviewed Phoebe's nurse and the two young girls. They then retired to write up their journal. The Nursing Sisters had to examine Phoebe and prepare her for burial. Once these formalities were complete, both groups met to compare notes and plan for the next step, which was a full meeting of the Sisterhood plus the two men next morning.

Helen opened the meeting with a short prayer for guidance.

'Phoebe's passing was nothing less than a triumph,' a ripple of surprise flowed through her audience. 'She made a full confession to us of her sins and we witnessed her experience the ecstatic relief of forgiveness,' Helen paused to allow her words to be absorbed. 'She then told us of a vision she had of an 'enlightenment' that had come to her.'

'We must do as Phoebe tried to do four score years ago and take the Sisterhood to a new land.'

Consternation rippled through those gathered.

'How? How can we possibly re-settle in a new land?' This call came from several of the oldest Sisters.

'We must have faith in Phoebe's vision,' Helen's voice sounded so strong and sure it reached all of her audience momentarily quelling the unrest. 'She said she would be the last to die on Luminos and would be part of the light that would bring the boat to take us away!'

'Where is 'away' was the general query of a most agitated enquiry. They were all upset.

'My first thought was that it would be the Abbey, even though we know it may soon be reclaimed by the original occupants.' Helen looked around at her audience; she definitely had their attention, but not their sympathy. Realising her role until now had been one of support to Phoebe, making her own character invisible, she took a more positive stance and determined to keep her tone strong and clear.

'Let us think about the events of the past twelve years.' Her new attitude seemed to settle her audience. 'Esma's group were given sanctuary here by the community at the Abbey. Four women and two children was a lot for us to absorb at the time as our spirit and strength were diminishing. But we found they brought an influx of vigour, plus the luxury of the supply boat coming every two years. If you recall the Abbey's boat was very old and Esma made an agreement that her boat could be used by the Abbey as long as we were regularly visited with supplies and transport back, if needed. The energy of Esma, Marla, Doris and Thele, plus the delight of watching Milla and Bebe grow up revitalised our community.' There were murmurs of agreement.

'Phoebe believed she saw a vision of herself and her sister as they were when they first travelled to the New Land, right at the moment Alphonse's body slipped into the sea. It was in fact Milla and Bebe exchanging places with the nurse for a short time which triggered Phoebe's vision, but that doesn't matter, it translates to the same thing.' Helen paused again, this time collecting her own thoughts.

'Phoebe agonised for a long time over us staying on Luminos. She grieved that we would die out once our home at the Abbey was no more. Then she believed we were sent the means of survival. Three shipwreck survivors were washed up on Luminetta. One we couldn't shift, the two we brought in have bonded and become part of our community. Phoebe knew the one we left behind would become a threat and watched for him from her window. Esma sensed his presence that last night and went to face him, Phoebe saw her leave and followed to help, but Luminos was his killer and Luminos saved Esma and Phoebe from the mortal sin of murder.'

'Phoebe died knowing her job was done. She had brought our Sisterhood together after the 'great disaster' sustained it for her lifetime, and now she felt it was ready to move on with Esma.' Helen turned to Esma.

'Now I ask Esma to tell us the full story of Alphonse.

CHAPTER FOURTEEN

Amid a stirring of interest, Esma rose to her feet.

'We came from Karakos,' she began abruptly, 'and I want to thank you all for never pressing us for details because if the merest whisper had got out, Alphonse would have found his way here to destroy us.' A general stirring of interest pervaded the audience, they all wanted to know about Alphonse.

'I was the only child of a dear man, a scholar, an academic who loved his books, medicine and the rule of law. He became a magistrate as well as a skilled physician. It was as a magistrate he visited Karakos. He loved the island, its open minded society, and decided to settle there. He bought a large tract of land and built a house and then a hospital. He envisaged devoting his later years to medicine after he retired, but that never eventuated.

As Chief Magistrate of Karakos, he was kept very busy. After Mother died, I seldom left his side, he took over my education, pleased that my interests were much the same as his own. He never married again and worried over my future. When he discovered he was terminally ill he became obsessed with securing my future. He chose Alphonse, a big strong, ambitious man with a good head for business. I didn't want to marry, but father thought it best for my protection.

He gifted me a generous dowry and made me the sole beneficiary of his estate but with an unusual proviso. Our home and hospital could not, in the case of my death or incapacity be passed on to my husband. It must instead be passed on to a hospital managing body, in particular the female society known as 'The Sisters of Light'.

In his travels prior to settling down he had received great help from a most obscure chapter of the Sisterhood that resided, temporarily, even then, at the Abbey. He never forgot. Father thought Alphonse would be happy with my fortune and I would be secure with a house and a hospital of my own. He was proud of my efforts in this field and thought my future would be safe.

Alphonse and I were married shortly before Father died. Immediately after he died, Alphonse took over my fortune. The funds that were needed for running the hospital became unavailable. Alphonse was clever enough to see to this piece of trickery, but I frustrated him by making do with whatever nature provided. Donations from grateful patients helped the hospital continue.' The ladies in the audience were only too familiar with 'making do' with whatever nature provided and privately applauded Esma for her efforts.

'The money I brought to the marriage was spent on a large boat. He called her the *Raptor Queen*. It was his pride and joy and he used it shrewdly. Bigger and faster than any other boat in the Karakos community, he devised a plan to collect the catch from the smaller boats and take them to market along with his own, for a fee. Without the trip to and from market the smaller boats could stay out longer catching more fish. Everybody won. The community as a whole became a little richer. More money to spend benefited the village and Alphonse was a hero.'

'My money also enabled him to purchase another wife. He wanted a son. We hated each other and barely spoke. Marla was a lovely young widow with a small daughter and her late husband's family were keen to contract a marriage for her to Alphonse. To them it was a welcome boost financially, as well as two less mouths to feed. Alphonse considered that as Marla had a daughter it proved she was not barren.

When no child eventuated, even after severe chastisements each time her cycle renewed, he sought another marriage. This time he chose sweet, innocent Doris and made a handsome offer for her. Her family were simple fisher folk and attention from Alphonse was considered an honour.

All the while, Alphonse's business life was booming, extending his interests beyond Karakos. Thele's husband Nikkos, at Alphonse's request carried cargo to one of the more north-easterly cities. One particular trip was to acquire some luxurious items for Alphonse's house. Thinking it more of a pleasure trip, he took along Thele and his little daughter, Bebe. The merchant they were visiting was enormously impressed with the two females, showering them with gifts and generous hospitality.

Hearing this alerted Alphonse to opportunity and he began exploring the possibilities of another wedding contract. This time he would be the recipient of the dowry.

No child had eventuated from Alphonse's three wives but he could vent his frustration by selling Marla's child, Milla. He knew I loved her as if she was my own and the thought of hurting me was too hard to resist. But it was Thele and Bebe who were wanted by the foreigners, so somehow he arranged to contract out all three. The fact the children were too young was a hurdle easily overcome. Just provide a clause to say 'no conjugal rights until they reached menstruation'. They would be so far away from us no-one would ever know if the contract was broken.

He considered this diabolical plan as fitting punishment for Marla for not giving him a son and a warning to Doris, plus I would lose respect for allowing this to happen. It was known that all Karakos women came to me when in trouble.' Esma paused for a slight breather; then pushed on.

'Nikkos had to agree because Alphonse had marked him as an ally for a long time. Exploiting Nikkos's greed and vanity, Alphonse advanced the money for Nikkos to buy a much larger boat. Then he added to the debt by encouraging him to buy a much larger house. Now very much in debt to Alphonse, Nikkos was worried. The plot, when first suggested, was rejected with distaste, but when his debt was asked to be repaid, he weakened. To be debt free and profit as well was too great a temptation, he agreed and they made plans.

Thele overheard the discussion and came to me. It was what subsequently led to our flight. Marla and I are both capable of handling a large boat. Navigation was no problem in local waters. Later when charting a new course, I found my father had taught me well.

I have often wished we could rally the Sisterhood and lay claim to the property on Karakos, but it always came back to the hard fact that the time wasn't right. Alphonse was too powerful being responsible for the new wave of prosperity in Karakos, he would have shut us down or worse.' Esma took a sip of water, eyeing her audience and assessing reaction. A deep flush of red now underlay Tomas's bruises, testifying to his emotional turmoil. Christos was cooler, no doubt wondering what next he would be called on to do. Thele, Marla and Doris were tense and fearful, and so too were the Old Sisters.

'No-one likes change,' she began, 'but if it provides a better, fuller, safer life, we must find the courage to take the chance.' There was a restless stir of anxiety.

'Phoebe decreed she would be 'part of the light' to lead us away and by that she meant she wished to be cremated on the pyre on top of Luminos.' She waited for the shock and horror to subside.

'This morning we have climbed to the top of Luminos and seen for ourselves the possibility.' She raised her voice louder to quell the growing protest, ending up beating her stick on the table.

'Standing at the top of Luminos, is like being in the middle of a saucer surrounded by a perfect circle of ocean. Phoebe's fire is going to take a lot of wood and I am going to call on Christos and Tomas to donate their stockpile and deliver it to the site, beginning today.'

'No,' cried Christos, loud and angry,' no, no, no! We have worked too hard!'

Tomas was dumb from shock but leapt to his feet in protest. He wanted to say something about the wood and planning how they would use it was all that had kept them sane, but his voice was too damaged from injury to carry above the noise. Esma beat on her table again.

'Christos! Listen to me!' She seemed to rise in authority but had in fact only stepped on a small stool to give her elevation. 'If we build a large enough fire and keep it going for as long as possible, it will be seen!' She thumped on her table to quell persistent mutterings. 'Once it is seen word will filter through to the Abbey. The Recording Sisters will confirm this method was used in the old days.'

'What did you use for firewood then!' shouted Christos.

'We had trees we grew for firewood and off-cuts from our orchard, but the firewood plantation disappeared in the earthquake. As you well know we use reeds and off-cuts for our fires now. They are not enough for the fire we need.' Esma grew more imperious as the argument proceeded.

'Once the Abbey hears of the fire on Luminos it will send my boat, the one I took from Alphonse, and it will take all of us back to the Abbey. It will take each of us back to where we want to go!' The audience was temporarily hushed as they grasped the idea and its implications.

'You can be taken back to your home, Christos. I know you are desperate for knowledge of your family.' Christos stood mouth agape. A way home had been offered, emotion overwhelmed him.

'You too, Tomas, if you have a home or anywhere else you wish to go you only have to speak.' Tomas couldn't speak, his emotions were too complicated. He had no home. Luminos was the first feeling of home he ever had, losing it would be unbearable.'

'Those of us who came from the Abbey can return if they wish or can come with me. I am returning to Karakos to claim my inheritance in the name of 'The Sisters of Light.'

CHAPTER FIFTEEN

Emotions were raw but the Sisters concentrated on the job in hand. There was a funeral to organise and Phoebe's wishes to be honoured, that was the priority.

'I didn't think you were so keen on building our boat!' Christos was surprised by Tomas's apparent consternation at the loss of their stockpile of wood. He too still coming to terms with the emotional shock, but was glad to feel he had the support of Tomas. He respected Phoebe and had a growing respect for the Sisters, but was also beginning to realise his dream of being able to build a boat to the standard necessary to escape this place, was far-fetched. It required faith to put his trust in the 'Light' and Christos' faith had always been self-belief.

'I didn't know it myself!' Tomas' feelings were in turmoil. It was a physical blow to learn Doris had been married to Alphonse. When earlier she mentioned taking 'vows' he thought she referred to the Sisterhood, instead they were marriage vows. The younger women weren't Sisters at all, they were refugees from cruel marriages. Now they are widows! It changed the situation entirely.

'I think we should give the 'Light' all the help we can.' Tomas was thinking aloud. 'We won't find a proper life here on this rock and if Phoebe has said the boat will come, then I choose to believe her.' He could barely suppress a rush of elation that was now threatening to burst out. If it did it would certainly upset the Sisters who were struggling to contain their grief and fear.

The two men set to with a will, clearing the area where the pyre was to be constructed, adjusting access in the parts where steps were broken or too steep for some to ascend. Esma wanted the fire to burn for as many days as possible so anything flammable was to be put out for collection which included old mattresses as well as their entire stock of wood. They used the fruit carts to transport these materials to the entrance of the passageway noting that possibly the carts too could be dismantled and burned if necessary.

Reed torches placed in the brackets along the walls up to the top of Luminos provided light and the Sisters formed a chain to help pass along all that was collected for the fire. Tomas and Christos were up and down the passageway more times than they could remember. Some items were too heavy for the Sisters to lift and assistance was needed. Some of the wood had to be cut down in size, but they toiled on relentlessly. The funeral had to be held at dusk next day and by late afternoon on that day, they were ready.

Despite being exhausted by the rigours of the past day and a half everyone presented themselves clean, tidy and well brushed just as the sun was going down.

Helen led the service with prayers and gave a touching eulogy. Esma spoke on behalf of the women of Karakos. Tomas and Christos were called on to be pall-bearers. Helen led the procession to the interment site, followed by Esma, then Phoebe, in her white robe, on a small litter carried by the men. The Recording Sisters followed and then the others with a younger Sister interspersed with the older ones to give assistance where necessary.

They all pressed well back as Phoebe was gently and reverently laid on her own bed, beautifully decorated with garlands of flowers, pretty shells and loops of beads made from coloured seeds, and set on top of the pyre. Once all was in order, the Sisters each came forward with a gift or personal memento to go with Phoebe into her next life. Some brought a prized trinket of their own. A scarf from Kaliope and socks from Ana two of the oldest sisters, sweet cakes from Milla and Bebe and a beautifully drawn up Testimonial created by the Recording Sisters and signed by the entire company. There was little room to spare, so it was decided that once the fire was alight they would all file past one by one to witness the most significant event since the earthquake devastated Luminos, then return to their community area for refreshment.

Tomas and Christos were in charge of lighting and maintaining the fire. They had set plenty of tinder at the bottom, lighter wood next to catch fire quickly, their heavy timber to create an up-draught and then Phoebe's bed on top. They thought she looked serenely beautiful lying there in her simple white robe, and as they approached with the torches to set the fire going, their emotional control cracked and tears streaked their faces.

Firstly, quickly the tinder caught, igniting the lighter firewood which scorched then burned the heavier timber exploding them into flames which flared upward to touch the edge of Phoebe's bed. Seeing the men's distress loosened the Sisters self-control and they all wept openly, some loudly, as they each filed past the fire. They needed the release of pain of loss and fear of the future. They cried all the way down the passage and continued until they reached their community area. Familiar surroundings soothed unfamiliar grief.

Tomas and Christos were left to cope with the horror of the interment. They did their best to keep the fire as intense as possible, but keeping it going did not diminish the acrid smell of smoke or the dreadful odour of burning flesh. They were scorched by the fire, appalled by the spectacle and sickened by the smell.

Hours later, the arrival of Helen, Esma and the Recording Sisters, with arms full of sweet herbs was a huge relief. The men were sent to refresh themselves and come back the next morning.

All through the night the women took turns to tend the fire. They covered Phoebe with rosemary and hot coals and added more wood. The next morning when the men reported for duty the fire still burned fiercely, but Phoebe's corpse was no longer obvious and the air although smoky, was sweeter.

'Do you think we should disassemble the fruit carts?' Tomas asked, only to be told they would be required for carrying goods to the wharf. The Sisters were now fully engaged in choosing what should be taken away when the boat came. They did not doubt it would arrive.

Foodstuffs formed most of their luggage. The food put down for the winter months would surely be welcome at the Abbey. Records kept of Luminos were tightly wrapped and sealed. Esma's medical notes, her father's papers and books, as well as her precious remedies and phials were packed. Everyone was given instructions on what they could take and how it should be parcelled. No matter escaped Esma's attention, she was very aware space could be at a premium should the boat that arrived not be her own. The Abbey, at Esma's request, had de-registered *Raptor Queen* and re-named her *The Light of the Sea*. It pleased her to give a beautiful boat a beautiful name and it made her feel more hopeful of the future knowing that *The Light* would not be stained by dark memories.

The fire raged for six days before it was reduced to a glow. The winds started to come heralding the change of season, and the ashes of the fire lifted and started to disperse. Work wound down and there was time for reflection and for worry. Frantic activity ceased, now there seemed nothing to do except wait. And that was harder than anything.

Kaliope, took it upon herself to climb the passageway to the pyre site every few days. She was fascinated with the view and the perfect circle of ocean you could see surrounding Luminos.

She wasn't looking for the boat or even thinking of it, she was enjoying the place, the vista and spiritually communing with Phoebe when she noticed a speck on the horizon. She stared at it for some time before it struck at her heart like an arrow. She gasped, covered her mouth with her hands in amazement, and hurried back down the passage.

'It's come!' she cried, tears coursing down her face. 'There is a boat on the horizon!'

CHAPTER SIXTEEN

News of the fire on Luminos had sent shock waves through the Abbey. Eleanor, the Abbess, immediately despatched a message to Edward of Styne. It would take the Abbey's boat about a week to reach Edward and then at least another for him to reach Luminos, assuming he could sail immediately.

When Esma and her group first sought sanctuary at the Abbey and found there was no harbour for her boat at Luminos, Eleanor suggested approaching Edward of Styne who represented the Free Society of Artisans and Stonemasons who in collaboration with the

Monks of St Edward built the Abbey some two hundred years ago.

'He may be interested in chartering your boat,' Eleanor had suggested. 'He often has need of one and uses ours from time to time. Perhaps it could even be of future benefit to the Sisterhood.' Esma took up her suggestion, further suggesting it be re-registered and re-named *The Light of the Sea*.

It was all quickly arranged and in the years since had worked smoothly. Eleanor changed the name of the boat and Edward kept it well away from the Abbey, only ordering the two-yearly run to Luminos with supplies.

As *The Light of the Sea* dropped anchor just off Luminetta excitement and dread were evenly mixed among the Sisters on Luminos. Every inch of the boat's progress toward the Rock had been monitored from the time it was first seen as a dot on the horizon. As soon as it was near enough Esma, Marla and two of the Recording Sisters rowed over to

Luminetta and were waiting on the beach to greet whom-ever came ashore. They noticed the rowboat carried two oarsmen and two officials.

Edward had never met any of the leaders of the Sisterhood at Luminos, over the years he had left the two yearly contacts to the Captain of *The Light of the Sea*. On this occasion, he thought it best to keep the boat fully manned whilst he and his carefully chosen partner Richard assessed the situation ashore. If it was a natural disaster no-one could handle it better than Richard, he was strong, athletic and cool-headed. To their surprise there were no visible signs of panic among the four women they could see standing on the sand. The men jumped ashore as the boat beached, wading the last few paces towards the group of women.

'Welcome to Luminos,' said the tallest one, stepping forward and holding out her hand. She was unlike anyone he ever imagined. Stark white hair, but not old, tanned skin but not weathered, she looked vibrant and healthy. Very bright blue eyes, the brightest he had ever seen, acutely penetrating, he felt he had been cut by a diamond. 'I am Esma of Karakos. This is my sister Marla,' she indicated a shorter, softer more curvaceous woman none-the-less one who exuded quiet strength, 'and these are two of our Recordists from the Sisters of Light.'

Edward introduced himself and Richard and easy conversation followed. Apparently there was no crisis that was not now resolved, they just needed their boat back.

'We have filled the cavern on this little island with all the food we laid down for winter, plus the personal belongings of our Sisters. These will need to be transferred to *The Light* and tomorrow beginning at low tide, we will ferry out all of the Sisters. There will be twenty of us altogether.'

'Does the Abbess know you plan on returning to the Abbey?'

'No, not yet, there is no way of communicating!'

'That is a lot of people for the Abbey to absorb!' Edward replied in concern.

'I am hoping it will be temporary,' Esma sounded sure and completely practical. Changing the subject she invited both men to dine with them this night. 'It will be our last meal on Luminos and as special as we can make it. We can accommodate you and your colleague. Your men can take your orders back to the boat to begin loading our goods. We will be ready to leave in the morning.'

Taken aback by her cool assumption of control, Edward hesitated, but Richard spoke for the first time.

'I would be very interested to visit Luminos. It intrigues me greatly and there is enough of the day left for us to have a good look around.'

Surprised again, Edward agreed to the invitation. His respect for Richard was deep and he knew there would be a solid reason for Richard to intervene.

They all boarded the Sister's boat, Marla and Esma manning the oars. The men offered to row but were turned down. 'There is a trick to it and it's better to observe first,' they were told. It was a breathless experience for the two men. They marvelled at the skill shown passing through the reef, then alongside the rock to the entry and then into the cavern and lastly drawing alongside the old stone pier.

It was an even greater surprise to see the Rock from inside the reef. They were invited to explore at will, speak to anyone they pleased and were given instructions to report at sundown for dinner.

CHAPTER SEVENTEEN

Leaving Luminos was slow, nerve-wracking and dangerous. At the end of the day they were all on board, physically and emotionally exhausted. The Sisters gathered in little groups around the deck staying put where they sat down.

Esma and Helen accepted the offer of the Captain's cabin as they had decided to sail straight for Karakos to make their claim without delay and needed privacy to work on a strategy.

Fortunately the weather held fine and cruising steadily en route to Karakos was like a holiday; something the Sisters had not previously experienced. They had their meals delivered to them, an unknown luxury. Tomas and Christos were responsible for collecting the meals from the galley. Esma had offered to donate to the ship's stores some of the food they brought aboard, but it was unnecessary.

'We have already loaded extra provisions,' Edward explained, 'and cook would rather adhere to his routine and not be troubled by adapting to different foodstuffs.'

It took a day or two to become accustomed to the boat and to get their 'sea-legs'. They had been offered the crew's quarters below deck, but that area was not only tiny and stuffy, they would have had to string up extra hammocks. The Sisters seriously doubted being able to manage hammocks so they opted to sleep on deck and to take their chances on the weather.

Tomas and Christos brought the sisters each their bundle. The ladies extracted a blanket and used the rest of it to sleep upon.

Two empty cargo crates were placed side by side at the back of the boat, convenient to where the Sisters were 'camping', a pail was placed inside each one and these were their make-shift latrines.

Their first breakfast was brought to them soon after dawn. Boiled or pickled meat, fresh bread and butter-biscuits, made up the menu. Tomas brought the food in two pails. Christos carried a kettle of tea and a pail of tin plates and pannikins. They liked the bread, biscuits and tea, but took little of the meat.

Dinner time there was roast duck, roast beef and ham in one pail and boiled turnips, carrots, potatoes and cabbage in another. The Sisters took a little more of the meat and good helpings of vegetables.

Tea time there was more of the same, this time with the addition of cheese. Most of them chose cheese to eat with the bread saved from breakfast and more tea. They were offered ale or a measure of wine or port, but these were declined. They had eaten more on their first day at sea, than in several days on Luminos and had done no work to compensate.

Tomas and Christos loved the fare. It was what was usually dished up on every boat they had worked on, but there was more of it and better quality. They embraced life at sea again, sleeping below decks with the rest of the crew and throwing themselves into whatever chore they were asked to do, as well as running around and looking after the Sisters. Their respect for the women was obvious and their attitude picked up and copied by the rest of the crew.

For most of the Sisters it was an uncomfortable but exhilarating adventure. When they heard they would be sailing straight for Karakos there was consternation, but their faith was in Esma, believing she would carry out Phoebe's vision. Among themselves they planned a show of support for Esma for when they left the boat.

The day prior to their arrival in Karakos, using their blankets, they curtained off a small area of the deck and washed for the first time in a week. Feeling clean, and well groomed, habits unwrapped and freshened in the air, their emotions stifled, they presented themselves united.

Tomas and Christos wanted to present themselves well too, but they had nothing other to wear but their brown habit. That would be unsuitable because they would certainly be called on for extra ship-board duties once they were in port. The best thing for them to do would be to keep out of sight and not embarrass the ladies.

Early the next day, just after breakfast, as Karakos loomed on the horizon they all wondered who would make the first move. Esma was wondering too and decided to be bold.

'Raise the Sisters' flag,' she ordered the Captain.

Displaying a full moon, with a cross contained within that moon, and cupped by two crescent moons depicted in white on a pale blue background, it was unlike any flag he had ever seen, but he raised it without hesitation.

Through the boat's eyeglass, Esma could see activity on the dock and crowds gathering on the beach. 'They all know this boat as the *Raptor Queen*! It will be a great surprise for them to see she is now *The Light of the Sea*.'

'It looks like an official party has arrived!' The Captain had taken over the telescope, but Esma quickly took it back.

'That is Alberos, the Chief Magistrate of Karakos!' Her voice lifted with excitement. 'I know him and he is a good man. He was Magistrate when we left Karakos. He took over from my father. We will get a fair hearing, of that I am sure! We must hurry and get ourselves organised.'

Around mid-day, *The Light* gently nudged the dock, lines were thrown down to fasten to the bollards and the crew efficiently set the gangway in place.

The Sisters confided their plan of support to Helen who went along with their gesture and led the column of white clad Sisters down the gangway. She then stood aside while they formed two lines with a Recording Sister carrying a chronicle, at the top of each line.

Holding a wooden despatch box Esma would pass through this guard of honour, followed by Marla and Doris together, then Thele who would walk alone, then the two young women, Milla and Bebe.

Together Esma and Helen would lead the way and the 'Guard of Honour' would fall in behind.

'We hope it will make us look united and purposeful,' said Ana, their spokesperson. It certainly aroused curiosity because most of the inhabitants of Karakos had never heard of the 'Sisters of Light' and had never before seen their flag. They did recognise the boat though and the new name drew a hum of comment.

What caused the most surprise and drew an audible collective gasp was Esma's white hair. They had known her as a vital young woman with thick, curly, auburn hair, much like her father and at the peak of her beauty. She still had the same aristocratic bearing, lithe movement and compelling looks, but was in many ways, unlike her former self. The unusual group came to a halt in front of the Chief Magistrate of Karakos who was standing in front of a cluster of officials so that he could address the newcomers.

'State your business, Esma of Karakos. We are interested to hear why you have returned so long after your abrupt departure!' He obviously remembered her well but Alberos gave no indication of his re-action to her return.

'I have come to report to you the death of Alphonse of Karakos and to claim that part of his estate that should eventually be transferred to the Sisters of Light, some of whom are with me today.'

'What evidence do you have to support your claim?'

'I bring you witnesses to his death, sworn statements of the event, the Chronicles of our Society, and my Father's Last Will and Testament which details how his house and hospital should have been disposed after his death.'

'It will take time to study your claims!' Alberos still gave no indication of his reaction to Esma's presence or indeed to that of her associates.

'Yes, I appreciate it will take time.' Esma felt her father's blood rising in her veins, he would never falter and neither would she, 'That is why I ask you to allow those who are with me now to take up temporary residence in my father's house, until you and the Council have had time to study these papers and to interview us all. I have my own set of keys.'

Alberos studied those assembled before him. He had no doubt of Esma's integrity. The sudden flight and years of hiding had obviously taken a great toll. His eyes softened as he gazed at the collection of gentle but determined women and wondered what harm it could do to grant their request.

'Are you mad enough to consider their proposal?' The angry shout came from Nikkos, Thele's husband and father of Bebe. 'She abducted my wife and child and scuttled my boat so that I could not give chase.' There was a stirring and murmuring amongst the crowd, the women's escape was well remembered as the single, most dramatic event in the history of Karakos.

Alberos considered Nikkos. True, it had taken him several months to restore his boat to sea worthiness but after that he had profited by taking over Alphonse's business operation. He was now the middleman in taking the collective catches to market for a price, leaving the smaller craft to continue fishing. Prosperity had been restored to the community and no thought given to Alphonse who had been driven mad by the ridicule.

To fund a search for Esma, Alphonse needed the money he had loaned Nikkos. Until the boat was re-floated Nikkos could not repay the debt. Too impatient to wait, Alphonse began scouring the seas by taking jobs on any boat he thought may sail in the direction she may have taken. There had been only a few sightings of Alphonse since then, all reported him obsessed to the point of madness.

Nikkos, on the other hand, had grown fat on the profits from Alphonse's usurped business, re-married and enjoyed a lavish lifestyle.

'Yes,' Alberos replied, 'I will consider their request. I too would like to get to the bottom of this matter.' Turning to Esma he added, 'You and your entourage may stay in your father's house. You will be contacted after the Council has convened.'

CHAPTER EIGHTEEN

Curious, the crowd stood mostly silent as the Sisters' entourage passed by on the way to Esma's home. Edward and Richard took it upon themselves to tag along behind forming a type of rear guard.

They wore their official dress, a light grey tabard bearing the insignia of St Edward over their usual dark grey outfit and looked strong, tough and professional enough to command respect. In fact the local men were confused by their presence wondering what 'was their role' in this surprising event.

Some of the women onlookers smiled fleetingly or nodded to Esma, but were careful not to make too much of a fuss. Most of the women had reason to be thankful for Esma's help in the past and were glad to see her return. Many of the men took the opposite view because of the theft of and damage to the boats involved in the scandal. Although once their livelihoods were restored, thanks to Nikkos, some of them reluctantly admitted Esma's hospital was missed.

Esma's home stood proudly on the coast overlooking the bay. Alongside it, but separated by a large lawn and neglected shrubs was the plainer, simpler hospital building. Coming up to it after so long, Esma felt herself overwhelmed by the emotion of being home and possibly having to leave again. She chose not to recognise uncertainty. 'Possession is nine points of the law' she told herself, determined that never again would she leave this place.

Placing her key in the lock of the front door and feeling the familiar 'click', she pushed it open.

It was dusty and untidy with all the signs of a careless and angry departure, yet it was still her home. Untouched for years, this haven of peace and scholarly endeavour had waited for her return and now she was here to bring to fruition her dreams of the past. Turning to face the group of women filling the forecourt of the house she addressed them with tears rolling down her cheeks.

'Marla and Doris know this house equally as well as I. They will allot rooms. You will all have to share as best you can. Tomas and Christos are bringing your bundles. There should be extra bedding and blankets in the storeroom. I will sleep in my father's study. Helen is invited to join me or to take my mother's sitting room which is adjacent. There is much work to do as I do not believe Alberos will keep us waiting too long before we are called before the Council.'

Esma's speech ended abruptly when she disappeared inside the building. After a little hesitancy the others followed, all milling around the unfamiliar reception room, which led to another very large room of which glimpses could be seen. Marla and Doris soon took charge.

Helen asked for directions to the study Esma had mentioned and found her pulling back heavy drapes, flooding the room with warm mid-afternoon sunlight.

'What are you planning to do?' she asked, at the same time looking around in appreciation of the grand old room. Books lined the walls from floor to ceiling, a handsome desk stood in front of the window. There was a fireplace and comfortable leather covered chairs placed nearby. It was dusty and needed a nourishing polish but still exuded her father's warm and scholarly spirit.

'Alphonse used this study after father died. I intend searching for any papers that may strengthen our case.'

'Then I will give you all the help I can,' Helen replied. 'Just give me your orders!'

CHAPTER NINETEEN

Edward and Richard followed the entourage all the way to the house and once everyone was inside they closed the gates and placed themselves each side of the entry as sentries. They were standing there when Tomas and Christos arrived towing a large cart full of the Sister's bundles. They watched the cart being unloaded with more than usual interest.

'Are you going back to *The Light*?' Edward queried as the two men returned to the gate.

'We haven't been told to stay here and the cart is borrowed and has to be returned to the dock,' Tomas replied.

Edward observed the two men looked unsure of themselves which was a sign of weakness when you are in a strange place. They also looked very ragged. Their clothes, Edward noticed were the same as those worn by the Sisters. The clothes looked alright on the Sisters, but not so good on the men, who had worked hard in them each day of the journey.

Are they the only clothes you have?' Edward asked.

'We have our thick brown habits which we wear at night for warmth, but not during the day, they are too cumbersome. The Sisters gave us these when they rescued us, as our clothes were too torn to be decent.' Tomas's forthright reply revealed his own innate decency.

Edward smiled to himself, thinking it was clever of the Sisters to dress the two men in women's clothing, it may well have saved embarrassing complications, after all Tomas and Christos were fine men one just hitting his peak, and the other still in his prime.

'Richard and I are uneasy about some of the male elements here on Karakos. I think the resentment felt at the time of women's escape has resurfaced and it would be wise to place a guard on the gate tonight. Take this note to the Captain of *The Light*. It is to tell him to double the watch on the boat at all times while we are in port, allow no-one on board unless they have orders from me. I am also directing him to issue you both with a full set of clothes. Not the Tabard, of course, you need to have taken the vow to wear that, but our uniform is a different matter and will suit you both. This note will also tell him to send us two additional men for guard duty at nightfall and to be alert for our usual signal should there be trouble. Report back to me as soon as possible.'

Tomas and Christos could not have been more thrilled. After months of menial labour grubbing around in dirt, gardening, picking fruit, smoking fish, 'women's work' you might as well say, as well as the indignity of wearing women's clothes, there was going to be change and some action! They hurried down to the boat, the cart rattling along behind them and were back at the gate in just over an hour. Being dressed like men raised their morale enormously, and somehow they had found time to shave and cut off their hair. They each looked totally different. Edward asked them to guard the gate while he spoke to the Sisters about carrying out an inspection of the property. Richard indicated he was heading west and wandered off in that direction.

Thele answered the knock on the door and just for a few moments Edward, a professional advocate and negotiator, completely lost track of what it was he was about to say.

Thele had caught his attention during the walk to the Esma's house, he admired her form, her graceful movement and, more than anything, her lovely colouring. Her daughter Bebe was very similar, so sweetly fresh and innocent. He knew their story, the Abbess had told him years ago, but seeing them in the flesh now and realising what they would have been like twelve years ago appalled him afresh at the scheme hatched between Alphonse and Nikkos. It was the purest form of evil to sell a beautiful young mother with her little daughter along with another little girl, this one taken from her own mother, to some wealthy Eastern potentate for his ravishment and indulgence.

Thele smiled at him, her lovely tawny, black lashed eyes reflecting that smile. Edward was lost in admiration of the courage these women had shown in defying their husbands and taking the law into their own hands.

'May I help you,' she asked quietly and her voice fell on his ears as soft as a whisper.

'Richard and I are concerned there are people in this town who may cause trouble while you and your Sisters are here, so we have set a guard on the gate and ask you not to open the door to anyone but me, Richard, Tomas or Christos. Meantime, Richard and I are about to inspect the property for security reasons. Would you please pass these plans on to Esma?'

He had found his voice after an embarrassing pause, but she didn't seem to notice. It was the first time she had seen Edward up close, he reminded her of the rock of Luminos, cast in the same stone. She sensed his strength.

'Yes, of course,' she answered. They smiled fleetingly at each other, it was only the tiniest flash of time, but universally ageless. 'Thank you, Edward.' She held out her hand. He took it and raised it to his lips.

'Until tomorrow,' he promised.

CHAPTER TWENTY

The summons to meet with the Council of Karakos came more quickly than expected. At the appointed time, everyone was seated in the Magistrate's Court waiting for Alberos to appear. He made his entrance with due ceremony and all stood to show their respect for the Chief Magistrate and his Council. He acknowledged their gesture and quickly got down to business.

'We have studied your evidence Esma of Karakos and accept that Alphonse of Karakos died by accident.' There was a hum of comment from those present.

'We have also contacted Alphonse's man of business who delivered his books to us and it clearly shows where the money has flowed. The dowry money has all been dispersed and also the money in the Hospital Account has all been dispersed, mainly used to purchase the *Raptor Queen*, plus two wives. There are now no funds available in these accounts. Two substantial loans advanced to a private person have been taken out against the house and hospital. These loans have not been repaid.'

Another hum of comment rumbled through the Court.

'As there is no Will of the late Alphonse, his estate will be distributed according to the law of Karakos. Alphonse of Karakos was the beneficiary of John, late Chief Magistrate of Karakos, Esma's father, who entrusted him to maintain the home and hospital for Esma until her death when the two properties are to be passed on to the Sisters of Light.

Therefore, Esma may take possession of these buildings once back taxes are cleared.

'May I speak, your Honour?' Esma stood up and the Magistrate indicated his permission.

'I have documents proving money was loaned to Nikkos with his boat put up as security and another larger loan against his house as security. Surely I may press for payment of these loans?'

'I see no reason why these loans may not be called in. If there has been no attempt to repay them over the last twelve years there will also be a considerable sum of interest to take into account.'

A great roar of outrage erupted from Nikkos who was standing at the back of the Court.

'I am not paying this abductor a single drachma!' But his protest was drowned out by Alberos pounding on the counter with his gavel and shouting for order.

'A debt is a debt!' shouted Alberos. 'If the documents are in order I decree they must be paid.' He ordered the Clerk of the Court to bring the papers to him for scrutiny. After what seemed an age, he was satisfied, the debt stood and Esma was free to pursue it. He then called a break for lunch after which the remainder of the matters would be settled.

So far Esma had her house and hospital, although mortgaged and with back taxes due, but there was a chance of getting some money. They were too nervous to eat lunch and just waited patiently for the hearing to be resumed. Once they were re-assembled, Alberos began without preamble.

'I have read the sworn statements regarding the reason why these women fled Karakos and have made enquiries of my own which substantiate their claims. You planned to hand them over to foreigners to become brides? What have you to say, Nikkos?'

'I was under Alphonse's spell and seriously in his debt, so could not refuse to help him.' Nikkos's bluster had evaporated. He knew Alberos wouldn't accuse him without proof and so was at a distinct disadvantage.'

'What reparation do you claim, Thele of Karakos?'

'All I want is to be divorced from Nikkos.'

'And you, Bebe of Karakos, what reparation do you claim?'

'All I want is to be disowned by Nikkos.'

'And you Milla of Karakos, what reparation do you claim?'

'I don't know if there can be any reparation for me as I was Alphonse's adopted daughter.' Milla spoke quietly, but she was heard and all those present in the Court were deeply touched by the pathos of the young girl's statement. The women were blameless, just unfortunate enough to be comely.

'Your comments have been noted, Milla of Karakos.' Alberos struck his counter with his gavel once more.

'According to the law of Karakos I call upon Nikkos to perform the rites of divorce and disownment before me, my Clerk of the Court and those present in this court willing to bear witness.'

Standing before the Magistrate and facing Thele, Nikkos repeated three times, 'I divorce you, I divorce you, and I divorce you.' Then standing before Bebe repeated three times, 'I disown you, I disown you, and I disown you.'

The Clerk of the Court took some time to collect all the witness' signatures to Nikkos's and Thele's divorce and the disownment of his daughter. It was the best bit of theatre the citizens of Karakos had ever seen and to be part of it was irresistible.

Alberos once more called the Court to order.

'It is the further ruling of this Court that the intended victims of this 'Sale of Brides' each receive damages in the sum of five hundred drachma. These damages are to be paid equally from the Estate of Alphonse of Karakos and from Nikkos of Karakos. There were uneasy murmurings while this judgement was being digested.

'Is there any other business? Alberos asked of those assembled when they all appeared settled.

'I would like to pursue repayment of the outstanding loans to Alphonse's Estate, Your Honour,' Esma stood quietly facing the bench.

'I flatly refuse to pay that woman anything!' Nikkos roared, red-faced and bullish. He had been thinking he might get out of this mess for his half of the damages and fudge his way slowly out of the rest. The house would have to go, but the boat he must keep.'

Order was vigorously called for and eventually restored.

'This Court will not be disrupted again. Another outburst and you will be held in contempt.' Alberos was livid with anger, the Court was not being shown respect, and he would not tolerate disrespect.

'I order you Nikkos of Karakos to repay the outstanding loans plus all accrued interest, plus reparation fee to the victims of your 'Sale of Brides' scheme, plus costs to this Court within ten days. Failure to do so will result in the seizure of your boat and your house. My Clerk will prepare the necessary papers. Court dismissed!' Alberos shouted and gave the bench an almighty bang with his gavel.

'Well! What do you think about that?' Edward asked of Thele who was sitting next to him. They were all back at Esma's house, stunned by the rapid change in their fortune. Some were making tea, others were handing around food. Villagers had called in bringing gifts of bread and cake and other things to eat.

'It changes everything,' she began, but was then called away. Edward wandered off outside and came across Bebe weeping in the garden. 'What is the matter?' he asked.

'I have been waiting for years to meet my father and the day I do he 'disowns' me without looking me in the eye, or showing the least regret.'

'I have always wanted a daughter,' Edward replied soothingly, 'but first I need a wife and it has taken forty years for the right woman to come along. If you would help me to convince your mother to marry me, then I could be your father and we would both be happy.'

'Are you serious?' Bebe was amazed. Edward assured her he was. 'Then I promise I will do all I can to help. I think you would be a lovely father,' Bebe said laughingly, kissing him on the cheek, but then a more serious thought crossed her mind. 'If I am going to convince my mother to marry you, I had better learn a little more about you. Where do you come from Edward?'

Esma, who was outside in the garden, heard this touching exchange, but did not make her presence known, she was quietly trying to come to terms with the events of the day. Nevertheless she was warmed by the knowledge there was romance in the air. Edward of Styne would be a good match for Thele and an understanding father for Bebe.

Moving away, Esma saw Christos, showing off his new clothes to Milla, he wasn't emotional after the Court ruling, but obviously liked the way Milla noticed him.

Tomas was looking for Doris. You could see he was bursting to show her his new look. When she did see him, she couldn't believe her eyes, standing and staring, her hands to her cheeks.

'Tomas! Is it really you? You look so handsome!'

It was as if the heavens had opened for Tomas, he couldn't believe his eyes or his ears. To see her undisguised admiration and to be called 'handsome,' was beyond his wildest imaginings. Robbed of his voice by overwhelming emotion, he simply opened his arms. She ran into them and was clasped close to his chest, feeling his wild heartbeat. He almost smothered her with kisses at first, but the paroxysm passed and he calmed down, holding her gently. Tomas had never been in love before, but he had all the natural instincts of a truly generous and patient lover. He waited until he felt her relax, until he saw a softening of her expression, until she raised her lips to his. This time he drew her into an embrace slowly and felt her respond and then they were both totally oblivious of everything, except this beautiful new life that was opening around them.

Esma left them all in peace. There was so much to consider. She wanted fulfilment for everyone. It would come, she decided, we just have to keep to a steady course for a little while longer.

CHAPTER TWENTY-ONE

Settlement of the Court's judgement took a lot longer than ten days to happen, but finally Nikkos's house and boat became property of Alphonse's Estate, and as he had died intestate and without issue, Esma was the principal beneficiary, with Marla and Doris as second and third wives in a proportionate share.

Bitter and broke, Nikkos left Karakos, taking his new wife with him.

Esma called a meeting with Marla and Doris. They were now the co-owners in varying proportion of two houses, one hospital and two boats. There needed to be money raised to pay off the back taxes owing on the properties and to pay the reparation ordered to Thele, Bebe and Milla, for the 'Sale of Brides.' Plus Edward was to be asked if his teams of Stonemasons and Builders could adapt their houses into suitable accommodation for the Sisterhood so there was permanent accommodation on Karakos for 'The Sisters of Light' from the Abbey.

'You will need some capital to get your projects started,' Edward advised, 'and I suggest you apply to the Bank of Karakos for a loan in the name of the Sisterhood, a religious group are usually treated more kindly than individuals.'

He also advised he would like to continue chartering *The Light of the Sea* for some time to come as he had plans of his own for the future. He would pay her direct for the charter of the boat and not Eleanor at the Abbey, as in the past. This meant Esma would have some immediate income to pay off a loan.

They began discussing Nikkos's boat and decided to ask Tomas if he would take charge of the boat and business, in an arrangement that would see him share a good income with the Sisters. Tomas was proud to be given the opportunity and set about taking over command of the boat, commencing work at once.

Then there was Nikkos' house to consider. They decided to use it for the oldest sisters, the ones past being actively engaged in hospital work. There was plenty to be done off-site such as blending tinctures, lotions and simple potions, herbs needed to be grown and harvested for these purposes. There was also mending, darning and knitting small items like mittens and scarves. That was just the start, women used to being busy always found something to do.

Esma also decided to offer the guest-house on Nikkos' property to Tomas and Doris in exchange for Doris overseeing the general housekeeping for the property and

Tomas, although being engaged on the fishing boat, would give a greater sense of security to the establishment.

Tomas wasted no time in proposing marriage to Doris and approached Edward to build them a little house once he had made some savings. Edward asked if Tomas had ever been back to Ambros where he was born. On learning no attempt had been made he offered to make enquiries when next in the area.

It was month's later when Edward gave Tomas a bank draft for four hundred drachma, signed by Solomon Rei, Banker, Ambros. It was a small sum in the overall scheme of things, but it was a huge boost in self esteem for Tomas. It represented the proceeds from the sale of his parent's possessions from the time he was seven years old, plus thirty-five years interest. He added it to his growing bank account in Karakos immediately and truly felt a man of substance. Doris had money coming, as did Marla, both from the settlement of Alphonse's estate, but both women chose not to draw on it until the hospital was well established.

Richard had exciting plans for a lighthouse on Luminos and asked Marla to join him and a team. He was waiting on Edward to approach different island communities for them to financially support the project. A lighthouse in dangerous waters would be of great benefit to people who fished for their living.

Marla wouldn't leave Milla, and Milla wanted to be with Christos so they took Christos to Yendruka at last. He found all that was left of his family was his widowed mother. She was waiting on the dock when *The Light* sailed in, as she had waited on the dock to meet every vessel since their family's boat went missing.

So overwhelmingly emotional was the re-union between mother and son, Edward and Richard invited her to come back to Karakos with them while they waited for the 'go ahead' for the lighthouse, and extended to Christos an invitation to join Richard's team on that project.

Edward spent the next several months sailing back and forth between the islands re-settling the Sisters from the Abbey as accommodation became available. As planned the oldest went to Nikkos's house and the more able to Esma's.

The first social celebration for the Sisterhood on Karakos, was the marriage of Tomas and Doris. It was a joyous occasion, held on the big lawn between Esma's house and the hospital. Invitation was spread by word of mouth and almost all of the villagers turned up to take part. So much was happening in Karakos, everyone was excited. Building work was progressing, the hospital was open and new people were arriving every few weeks.

A short time later Edward approached Alberos and asked if the Council had a suitable place for him to reside temporarily, as he could see he would be engaged with business on and around Karakos many months more and he wanted to marry Thele. The Old Customs house was suggested, which needed a coat of whitewash, but had lovely views of the harbour. In no time at all it was ready, and the Sisters were busy preparing another wedding feast.

'My father is retiring and I am taking over management of our family estate.' Edward explained to Thele. 'I intend taking you and Bebe with me to Styne, and I want us to be comfortable as a family when we arrive.

You will have much to do to outfit yourself and Bebe, and living apart will allow you to concentrate on your preparations. Styne is very different from living with the Sisterhood, but I am sure you will like it. Richard will take over my work.'

Their wedding and reception was a small, dignified affair but the villagers were waiting outside for the newlyweds and followed them all the way up to the Customs House. They watched as he elegantly handed his bride down from the open carriage and escorted her up the path to the front of their charming old house, where a servant stood inside the door. Reaching the veranda they turned to wave goodbye to their well wishers, but no one made any move to leave.

Having a good sense of theatre, Edward drew his bride to his side and kissed her warmly, but not overly long and then ushered her through the doorway of their home to the rousing cheers of the assembled well-wishers. The servant closed the door and satisfied, the crowd dispersed.

Finally financial support came through for the Lighthouse on Luminos. There was a flurry of activity assembling the team, getting equipment together, going over plans again.

Richard and Marla and Milla and Christos decided they wanted to marry, pleasing Christos's widowed mother, whom they were taking with them and whom the entire team called 'Nonna'.

Alberos conducted the double ceremony in the Court-house and there was a raucous send-off at the wharf when *The Light of the Sea* sailed once again for Luminos.

'We can quarry that rock,' Richard had explained to Edward, back when they had been gazing at the huge piece of granite that blocked the entrance to the harbour of Luminos, and use the stone to build the light-house. It will be hard, but not impossible.'

EPILOGUE

Seven years later the work at Luminos was done. Edward had overseen the re-settlement of all involved from the Abbey, Karakos, Ambros and Yendruka, and still using *The Light of the Sea* brought the main participants back to see the big Light being turned on. They were to be joined, en route, by the officials representing the group of islands who put up the money for the construction of the lighthouse. They were the ones who chose the French built magneto-electric generator because it had been found to work with great steadiness and good efficiency. They also decided to go with the newly invented tungsten filament light bulbs invented by Thomas Edison, as many lighthouses were now changing over to these bulbs.

It was an amazing sight to see two boats moored side by side in the ancient harbour.

It was to be *The Light's* last voyage for the group, she was retiring to be a 'hospital' ship, fulfilling Esma's dream of bringing medicine to the islands.

Christos and Milla now had enough money to purchase a sturdy boat to service the supply needs of Richard's team. Christos's old home at Yendruka had been made into a depot, making that place the centre of their activities.

Richard had also drawn up plans for two fine cottages to be constructed on Yendruka big enough to accommodate their growing families. Construction was due to begin once the lighthouse was completed.

Christos and Milla had three little boys and Richard and Marla were expecting their first child very soon. Nonna was thrilled with all this activity as she could see her beloved island coming to life again.

Tomas and Doris were proud parents of a boy whom they named Leo because he was so fair and strong. Three years later a little girl arrived, she looked so like her brother they called her Leoni. Tomas adored his family, but the little girl could wrap him and her brother, around her tiny finger.

He had been asked to Captain *The Light* in her new role. It pleased Tomas because it would not be as physically arduous as the fishing boat and he would have more time with his family. They were his all. He also wanted a nice home for them and with this in mind he approached Edward and asked if he would support his bid for the old custom's house now that Edward and Thele and Bebe would be permanently shifting to Styne. It was to be a surprise for Doris.

Edward was pleased to oblige and negotiated a very reasonable price for the house. Tomas wanted his home to be the first thing he saw when he returned to harbour from his trips away and the last thing he saw as he left.

Edward too was secretly hoping for a more stable life. Thele and Bebe had adjusted to life at Styne with ease, but always accompanied him on his trips back and forth to the different islands. Bebe had drawn plenty of attention from local admirers at Styne and confided she was ready to accept a proposal of marriage from one particular young man, should it eventuate. Edward was very aware it was time for them all to settle down.

Those who knew Luminos, were amazed when *The Light of the Sea* was able to navigate its way through a narrow passage into Luminos Harbour and moor at the old wharf. No longer was it necessary to unload offshore alongside Luminetta.

Charmingly picturesque little stone cottages, built to shelter the construction workers, lined a roadway that was once the path to the entrance of the rock. These cottages would now accommodate future workers at the Lighthouse.

The Sisters caves had become part of the building site. The general area where the Sisters used to cook and gather could still be used for social purposes.

They stood there now, around the base of the construction awe struck at the cleverness of Richard and his men. Up close the building was absolutely huge and they voiced their admiration to Richard.

'The building of the actual light house was arduous, I admit, but not as difficult as quarrying the rock. That in turn was easier than installing the magneto-electric generator to power the light. One little slip-up could have ruined years of back-breaking labour.'

Richard spoke eloquently, thanking all involved with the construction. He thanked those who provided the finances, for having the foresight to see that by using the best available equipment to make these waters safer, would expand local economies and help surrounding communities to prosper.

'We have called her Phoebe's Light,' he said, looking at those around him. 'She was the guardian of this rock, Luminos, and gave it her life. Now her guardianship will continue to provide guidance and safe harbour to those at sea,' and with that Richard pressed the button that started the generator that switched on the light.

Standing on the deck of *The Light* as she negotiated her way out of the harbour, Esma was brightly illuminated with regular flashes from the great lamp. Her face was shown to be tight with emotion.

'What are you thinking of Esma?' Helen asked.

'Phoebe,' was her surprising reply. She took a few minutes to compose herself before continuing. 'She made amends for her sins and was forgiven. We were both witnesses to that event, but that great light seems to suggest to me she is still waiting for something.'

'I don't understand!' Helen replied.

'The baby she left at the orphanage,' Esma declared, 'I feel she still wants to know the baby's fate.'

'Perhaps she does, now,' Helen replied quietly. 'Sadly, we will never know. Phoebe came to the Abbey alone, a life time ago. Before that she and her sister had been to the 'New World' as she admitted to us. I understood, from what was recorded in our chronicles that was how we described Australia. If the child survived and I think she would have done, if she was anything like her aunt, then she would have lived a good life, under southern stars.'